Summer's Shadow

Anna Wilson lives in Bradford on Avon with her husband, two children, two cats, one dog, six chickens and a tortoise called Hercules. She spends as much time as she can in Cornwall, and her time there inspired this vividly written stand-alone novel.

Also by Anna Wilson

For younger readers

The Poodle Problem
The Dotty Dalmatian
The Smug Pug

Monkey Business
Monkey Madness

I'm a Chicken, Get Me Out of Here!

The Puppy Plan
Pup Idol
Puppy Power
Party Party

Kitten Kaboodle
Kitten Smitten
Kitten Cupid

www.annawilson.co.uk

Summer's Shadow

Anna Wilson

MACMILLAN CHILDREN'S BOOKS

First published 2014 by Macmillan Children's Books
a division of Macmillan Publishers Limited
20 New Wharf Road, London N1 9RR
Basingstoke and Oxford
Associated companies throughout the world
www.panmacmillan.com

ISBN 978-1-4472-4181-2

1 3 5 7 9 8 6 4 2

A CIP catalogue record for this book is available from
the British Library.

Printed and bound by CPI Group (UK) Ltd, Croydon CR0 4YY

*To 'the rocks' – a beautiful
place of endless inspiration*

Prologue

Summer was asleep when the phone rang. She heard the shrill noise as though from far away; her body and brain slow to respond. She resisted the ringing as it tugged her out of the comforting depths of sleep.

Someone else will answer it.

The sound continued, like an alarm.

Summer groaned, shifted, rolled on to her side and scrabbled to find the switch on the bedside lamp.

Fumbling with the tangled sheet, she freed her legs and slid out of bed. The summer was one of those freak heatwaves; the kind the Met Office loved to term a 'barbecue summer' – which was fine if you liked barbecues. Not so good if you had spent stifling days sitting by a hospital bed. Watching and waiting.

Jess's mum had apologized to Summer for the stuffiness of the house. 'It's these terraces – they trap all the heat. I've not given you a duvet, just a sheet. Hope that's OK?' She had fussed constantly from the minute Summer had arrived to stay with them. Her fussing was as suffocating as the heat.

1

Why isn't anyone answering the phone?

The ringing seemed to become louder and more urgent.

'All right, all right, I'm coming!' she muttered, shuffling towards the bedroom door.

She stopped, realizing she was walking away from the noise. She rubbed at her eyes fiercely.

It wasn't the house phone. It was her mobile. Her mobile which she had turned off before going to bed, as she always did. Her mother insisted on it. 'Screen time' was something they often fought over.

Wouldn't mind an argument with her now over stupid things like that.

The glow from the phone was unearthly, its 'vibrate' mode adding to its alien appearance as it jumped and shuddered on the windowsill. It rang and rang.

A jolt of panic surged through her.

It'll wake everyone!

She was fully awake now. She grabbed the mobile and saw the word 'unknown' the second before she answered.

'Hello?'

Silence.

'Hello?'

Summer glanced at the bedside clock. Only a few minutes to go before midnight. 'The magic hour', her mum had jokingly called it, when a smaller, younger

Summer had crept into bed with her, snuggling down after a nightmare.

Summer shook her head. These images of Mum had been swimming in and out of her mind ever since the accident, as though she were preparing herself, stocking up on memories, just in case.

She shook her head again.

Mustn't let myself think like that.

Still nothing from the phone. Summer swallowed, her throat dry, her tongue sleep-logged.

'Hello?' She was irritated now.

Great, a prank call.

Summer made to turn off the phone and crawl back to bed.

The voices reached out to her, distant at first, as though under water or at the end of a long, dark tunnel; snatches of muffled conversation.

'Hello?' she repeated. Less annoyed than fearful now.

Still only those watery voices. Her heart banged in her ears. She shifted the phone to try to listen more closely. Then, from among the crackling white noise and eerie chatter, came something else. Faint. Very faint.

'Bye, love.'

A familiar, throaty laugh rippled down the line. As though the caller were joking with someone in another room.

'Hello? Mum?' Summer's tone was urgent, pleading.

Bye, love. As though she were popping to the shops. *Back in a minute. Back before you know it.*

Summer was shouting now, all concerns of waking Jess and her family forgotten in her panic. 'Hello! Hello! Mum! It's me!' She would know that, wouldn't she? Mum had called *her.*

Then there was nothing again: or at least, nothing but the hissing, popping static.

Summer lowered the phone and stared at it. She looked over at the clock again. One minute to midnight now. She put the phone back up to her ear.

'Mum?' Summer choked, her voice thick and salty.

There was a gentle *click* and the connection was broken.

Summer shook the phone, pressed the buttons, all of them, any of them, to try to get the call back; shouted, 'Mum! Mum!' over and over.

Nothing.

She pressed 'call back'. The screen remained blank. Frantic now, she whizzed through the list of received calls. There was no number listed that she did not already know. No sign of an unregistered number even.

So. Definitely a prank call. Must have been.

Impossible: it would have shown up at least as an unknown number.

Summer's hand quivered as she replaced the phone on the windowsill. She slumped against the wall and slid down so that she was sitting with her back to the radiator beneath the window, its metal frame cold through her T-shirt.

She told herself, sternly, to get a grip.

Mum's in hospital.

She was on a ventilator, tubes and drips coming out of her like tentacles. She couldn't lift the phone to make a call. She couldn't talk the last time Summer had seen her. Didn't know her own daughter. Didn't know anything any more.

Summer cursed herself for not having the phone number for the hospital stored in her mobile. Jess's mum would have it in hers. But Summer knew she couldn't go creeping around the house at midnight trying to find it. She wasn't going to wake anyone to tell them about the call either.

They'd give me that look with their heads on one side. All concerned. They've been looking at me like that anyway. Since the accident.

She sighed, shuddering. The phone was not going to ring again. She pushed herself up off the floor and went back to bed.

She turned out the light and lay completely still, on her back, staring at the shadows cast from the street lights, listening to the house shifting and creaking in the heat.

Did I dream it?

She thought afterwards that she must have lain awake for a long time. In any case, she did not remember falling asleep before the light crept in around the edges of the curtains. A glance at the clock told her it was 5 a.m. Had she really lain there, staring and listening since midnight?

Someone tapped on the door. 'Summer?' A whisper, as though unsure whether to wake her or not.

'Yes?'

The door opened and Jess's mum peered through. 'I – I'm so sorry, Summer.' Her face was anxious, her kind eyes ringed with red, her soft, blonde hair bed-ruffled.

Sorry for what?

'It's all right, I was already awake,' Summer said.

Then she saw how her friend's mother clutched at the doorframe, how she seemed uncertain whether to enter the room.

Her chest lurched. She sat bolt upright.

'NO!' she shouted. 'NO! It isn't true. I SPOKE to her.'

Rachel took a step towards her, but seemed to think better of it. 'The hospital rang a couple of hours ago. I wanted to let you sleep for a bit longer . . .' She broke off and frowned. Then: 'You *spoke* to her? When?'

Summer was rigid, sobbing; tears and snot mingling in a hot wet film, blurring her vision, pinching her voice, causing it to rise. 'It was *midnight*. She *called*. I thought it would *wake* you. I thought . . . It rang and *rang* . . .'

Jess had appeared behind her mum. She saw her friend's distress and rushed to Summer's side, throwing her arms around her, crying herself now.

Jess's mum was shaking her head, her eyes glassy, her mouth crumpled. 'No,' she said quietly. 'You must have been dreaming. You know she couldn't have called you. And certainly not at midnight because . . .' She paused. Her lips trembled. Then, with a shuddering breath she said, 'Cat died. At one minute before twelve. That's what they said: "Time of death 23:59."'

Summer saw herself push Jess aside, run to the window and pick up her mobile. Saw her arm jerk forward as she hurled the phone against the wall. Heard it shatter.

Heard herself scream.

Chapter One

It was the will which changed everything.

'I, Catherine Jones, appoint Tristan Trewartha of Bosleven, St Gerran, Cornwall to be the sole Executor of my Will and the sole Beneficiary of my Estate. If my child, Summer Lamorna Jones, survives me, I appoint Tristan Trewartha as her guardian.'

That was it. Two sentences written by her mother, spoken by a stranger. Two sentences of cold impersonal words over which she had no control, no say whatsoever.

In a whirlwind of preparation, packing and farewells, Summer found herself on a train out of Paddington, heading for Penzance. She had checked it out on a map and been appalled when she had seen how far away it was.

'It's right at the bottom of the country! Almost as far as you can go,' she had said to Jess. 'And then this Bosleven place isn't even in Penzance – look!' She had traced her finger along the southwest coast line and stopped at a small cove where the village of St Gerran was marked.

'Land's End,' Jess had said quietly. She pointed to the tip of England, a couple of centimetres to the left on the map.

The train journey was so long. Rachel had told her it was nearly three hundred miles from London to Penzance. Talking about it had been easy: experiencing it was very different. She was trapped. Stuck on the same train for five, slow hours with only her iPod and a magazine for company. Going all the way; to the end of the line.

She closed her eyes and ran through the events of the past couple of weeks; they were as unreal to her as if played out by actors on a stage. Who were these people hugging her and offering empty words? They could not be the friends she thought they were if they were happy to hand her over to a family she had never met before, never even *heard* of.

'She must have trusted them,' Jess's mum had tried to reassure her. 'Tristan sounded lovely when I spoke to him. He has a wife called Becca and a son. You're going to a good family, I'm sure.'

How *can you be sure?*

'If he was so special to Mum, so *lovely*, why wasn't he at the funeral? Why has he never been to visit us with his *lovely* family? Never asked us to stay in his *lovely* house?' Summer had thrown the questions like spears.

Jess's mum had reddened. 'I – I don't know . . . All I know is they're your uncle and aunt. It's better that you go to be with relatives.' She had sighed, exasperated. 'I can't do anything about this. I'm sorry. I don't suppose your mum ever thought she would . . .'

'Die,' Summer had said. 'Go on, say it!'

Why am I being such a cow to her?

'Summer . . .' Jess had tried to intervene, but Summer pushed her away.

She had not been able to stop shouting, being horrible. It had been easier than giving in to how she really felt – that she wished it had been her in that coffin instead of her mum.

'My *uncle and aunt*? For crying out loud! Why don't I *know* them? Why can't I live here?' she had cried.

Jess's mum had made a conscious effort to sound controlled. 'I wish you could, Summer. But if your mum had wanted you to stay with us, she would have said.'

Summer opened her eyes as a large man struggled into the aisle seat next to hers. The train had stopped at Exeter. She already felt as though she had been travelling for hours.

She turned away from the man, wrinkling her nose as he unwrapped a burger, packed with fried onions and oozing ketchup. Summer's stomach churned.

She had not been able to face food for days, had had to force herself to swallow the careful meals Jess's mother had put before her.

11

'You've got to eat,' Jess had said.

'What's it to you?'

Summer found herself hardening towards her best friend and her family as she watched them accept her fate and go about organizing her departure. Jess, in her turn, had withdrawn, backed away from the lashing out and the hasty words which poured out of Summer, unchecked.

'So you're just going to let your mum hand me over to these people like – like a parcel?' Summer had demanded, as the day to leave drew closer.

Jess's eyes had welled up and she had turned away.

Her mother had tried to pacify Summer. 'Your mum was my best friend. I trusted her judgement. It's true, she never talked about family. Look, it's not as if I didn't ask her over the years, out of pure nosiness! She always made it very clear she didn't want to talk about family. In the end I had to respect that.'

Summer had not wanted to listen. 'Too right she never said anything about family,' she had snapped. 'It was always, "It's just you and me, Summer! Just you and me."' As she had sung the words out, her face had crumpled again. 'Not any more.'

Jess's parents had become businesslike as the days rolled by, calling Summer's new guardian, Tristan, on the phone, talking things through with him.

Summer had watched as her life spiralled out of her

control. She had tried to imagine what her uncle would be like. She had a snapshot of him that he had sent: a slim man with ruffled, dark hair and a shy, lopsided smile. At least he didn't look like a monster.

He hadn't sounded like one either, when she had at last plucked up the courage to speak to him herself. His voice was deep, smooth, refined like a radio newsreader's.

The conversation had been stilted. He had offered his condolences, chatted haltingly about his home, his family ('We have a son. Kenan. So you'll have someone your own age'). He had been at pains to make it clear how welcome Summer was.

Summer had responded with monosyllables at first, her brain buzzing with so many questions, she was incapable of asking any of them.

Who are you? Why don't I know you? How does your son feel about me coming to live with you?

Instead she had remained quiet and listened to him.

'So Monday then,' her uncle had said finally. 'No time like the present! Yes, er, great place to spend the summer holidays, down here . . . Right, well, I'll come and pick you up, of course. It's a long way from London . . . We can get to know each other on the journey! Lots to talk about!' There was a forced note of jollity in his voice.

Summer had insisted on getting the train, however, surprising herself at her boldness.

'Penzance, right?' she had said. 'That's what they told

me. I've seen it on the map. I *am* fourteen. It'll be easy. It's direct, isn't it? No changes. So. Jess's parents can help me book the train, make sure I get on the right one and stuff.'

'Well . . . if you're sure,' Tristan had agreed. All too readily, Summer had thought. He had actually sounded relieved. 'I'll send you money for the ticket, of course.'

She had expected him to protest, to say she was too young to travel alone. She did not know why she had so rashly said she would go there under her own steam: she had never taken a train out of London on her own before. Her mum had only ever let her do short journeys on the Tube.

But then, no one was acting normal.

Before she left, Jess had made a last-ditch attempt at showing she cared.

'You all right?' she repeated, on a loop, a nervous grin fluttering on her lips.

Yeah, I'm all right. My mum's dead and I'm going to live in the back end of nowhere with some relatives I've never even heard of before. I'm so happy I could dance.

Not long ago, Summer would have told Jess everything. Told her how frightened she was, how she could not stop thinking horrible thoughts.

This guy – how do I know he's for real, Jess? Has anyone actually, properly checked all this out? What d'you reckon, Jess, would you trust him?

14

Everything's moving too fast – I just feel so lost!

Instead she had routinely responded to her friend's repeated question with a small smile and a nod. 'Yeah, I'm fine. Everything's fine.'

Jess had looked relieved when she had finally said goodbye.

Now Summer was alone.

She stared out at the dark landscape rushing past the window. If she cupped her hands to block out the light from the carriage, she could just make out the horizon in the gloom.

'Cornwall is so beautiful.' If I had a quid for every time someone had said that to me recently, I'd have enough money to buy my own place wherever I wanted.

A voice broke into her thoughts and through the music she was listening to.

'Penzance, this is Penzance. Your final station stop. This train terminates here. All change, please, all change.'

She crammed her iPod into the top of her small rucksack, went to fetch her cases from the luggage rack at the end of the carriage and made her way off the train with the few passengers that were left.

End of the line. All change.

Couldn't have put it better myself.

Chapter Two

Summer stepped down from the train. The cool night air hit her and she shivered.

The station was not well lit. It took a few seconds for Summer's eyes to adjust after the strong glare of the train carriage. She followed the straggle of passengers along the platform to the station concourse, watching as people were recognized by friends and loved ones; waving, laughing, hugging, kissing. She looked around, trying to find a man who matched the snapshot in her pocket. Would her aunt and – what's-his-name – Kenan have come too?

Eventually she spotted a lean, tall figure, leaning against a pillar, his arms crossed. No one rushed to greet him.

That him?

She stopped to pull the photo out of her jacket, peered at it in the half-light, then glanced back at the man.

It was him. He had the same thin face. He was not smiling as he had been when the photo was taken: now sharp cheekbones gave him a hollow look and his dark eyebrows were locked in a scowl. His thick mop of equally dark hair was as unruly as in the photo though. He was wearing a worn, checked shirt and a pair of very shabby trousers that appeared to have a hole below one knee. A raincoat was slung over one arm, pinned to his chest.

Summer hesitated. Then he noticed her and waved uncertainly with his free hand. The shy, lopsided smile from the photo broke the scowl, softening his features, widening his eyes. She took a step towards him, torn between relief that someone was there for her and a wish that she could make a run for it instead; hurtle across the concourse, out of the building and away.

I could. I could get back on the train. Hide in the loo. Wait until it turned back to London . . .

He nodded at her, putting his hand in his hair and ruffling it in a sharp, awkward movement.

'Summer,' he said, as if stating a fact.

'Yes.'

'You look just like your photo.'

'Er, yeah. You too,' Summer said.

'You must be exhausted. Here, let me help.' He wrestled into his coat and then made to take her cases. He paused, looking her up and down questioningly. 'Is this it?' he asked, nodding at her luggage.

Summer bristled, tiredness making her tetchy. 'Yes. It's OK. I can manage.' She gripped the handles of her luggage harder. Her whole life was now crammed into

17

the two bulging suitcases and one little bag.

Tristan took the largest case, in spite of her protests, and said, 'Come on. The car's over here.' He turned and made for the exit.

Orange halos of light glowed from the lamps in the car park, illuminating the fine silver needles of rain. Summer felt them brush her cheeks and hair.

'Not Cornwall at its best, I'm afraid,' Tristan said, turning to face her as he opened the boot of his estate car. 'It chops and changes pretty quickly down here though. Glorious weather yesterday.' He stopped. 'Sorry. You don't want to listen to me babbling on.'

He heaved the case he had taken into the back, took the other one from her and loaded that too. Then he went to open the front passenger door before she had a chance to slip on to a back seat.

'In you get.'

She did as she was told, reluctantly.

I'll have to talk to him now.

'Feel free to sleep,' Tristan said, however, sliding into the driver's seat and slamming his door. 'It's a good half-hour from here, I'm afraid.'

Summer reached back to sling her rucksack on to the back seat.

'How far is St Gerran from Penzance?' she asked, remembering the address she had been given. 'I couldn't really tell from the map.'

Tristan shot her a glance as they waited at the traffic lights.

He laughed lightly. 'I'd say it's near enough. I drive in most days. It's our nearest town anyway. Unless you count Newlyn. But there's more happening in Penzance. Not that that's saying much!'

Summer said nothing.

Tristan coughed nervously. 'All I mean is, it'll probably seem very quiet to you down here, after London.'

They drove in silence through the town. He was right about it being quiet, Summer thought, as she took in her new surroundings. She saw only three people walking along the promenade.

OK, so it's raining and it's late – wouldn't stop people back home from going out, though.

She slouched down and rested her head against the cool window. Her eyes felt raw, her forehead hot. She was so tired.

'It's, er, it's pretty quiet at home too, just now,' Tristan said suddenly. He sounded awkward.

Summer glanced at him, but he was concentrating on the road ahead.

'I told you about your aunt and cousin on the phone?'

'Yeah. Becca and Kenan?' She took a deep breath, the words bursting out before she had a chance to think. 'If you're my uncle, and your surname's not the same as mine, is your wife my mum's sister?' She immediately felt stupid. Her mother would surely have mentioned a sister.

Didn't tell me about an uncle and aunt, though.

Tristan cleared his throat. 'I'm – er – I'm more of a *distant* uncle.'

'When did you find out about me?' Summer pressed on; now she had started, she might as well continue.

Tristan hesitated before answering. 'The solicitor got in touch after – after your mother. . . had her accident.'

Anger flared up in her. 'What? You didn't know about me before mum *died*?'

Silence. She had embarrassed him.

Well, why couldn't people just come out and say *it?*

The scene of her mother's accident flashed before her. She had been knocked down by a car. In front of Summer. The car had rammed into a low wall after it had swerved, its bonnet crumpled. Steam had gushed out of it. The driver had been flung forward on to the horn. It had blared out, once, sounding like an alarm into the stifling London air, before the airbag had inflated, saving him.

Nothing could save her mother. It had happened so quickly. She had lain there, as crumpled as the car, blood trickling from her nose, pooling on the road behind her head. So much blood . . .

Those days in the hospital had been a stupid waste of time. Those tubes, those machines emitting constant high-pitched noises. Empty promises that they were doing 'everything they could'. Cold, mechanical lies.

Eventually Tristan broke the silence. He made a small, apologetic noise. 'I, er . . . I am sorry for your loss.'

Summer seethed at the useless words. 'Yeah, you said. On the phone,' she snapped. 'So how come you didn't ever call her? Come and visit? Or at least come to the funeral?'

'I – I wasn't invited.'

'I don't get it—' Summer persisted.

'It's a little complicated. I'll explain another time,' he interrupted. 'When you're not so tired and, er, upset.'

'So—'

'I'm sorry,' he cut in. 'I am. Really. About all of this. We – I want you to feel at home. You are my family and I will look after you . . .' He gave a frustrated sigh. 'As I was saying, I told you about your aunt and cousin on the phone. Well, I'm afraid you won't meet them tonight. Which is probably no bad thing as I am sure you are desperate to get to bed. Anyway, Becca had to . . . to stay to look after Kenan. He said he wanted an early night. End of term and all that, I suppose. He goes to boarding school. Pretty shattered when he comes home. You'll see him in the morning. Probably late, though – you teenagers do love a lie-in!'

'Boarding school?' Summer said. 'Is that where I'll go?'

Tristan started. 'I . . . we haven't thought about school yet,' he stammered.

You haven't thought about me at all, have you?

'We'll need to talk about it, of course. You'll have to look at a few different places. There are schools around here. It's just . . . Kenan didn't, er, fit in . . .'

Summer closed her eyes against his nervous chatter. The idea of a new school on top of a new family overwhelmed her.

A whole new life. A whole new me.

'Mind if I put the radio on quietly?' Tristan said.

Summer shook her head without opening her eyes.

Tristan pressed a button and the sound of strings swelled mournfully through the car.

Her mother had always listened to classical music, flicking over impatiently whenever Summer had the radio tuned to her preferred stations. 'It's *real* music,' she would say, when Summer complained.

Summer kept her eyes closed, tried to let the music transport her, to find a place in her mind that was far away from the present. She wanted only to sink into a black, bottomless pit of oblivion; to not think, not talk, not listen to any more of her uncle's empty words.

Chapter Three

Summer twitched and woke to find she had dribbled on to her denim jacket. Thank goodness it was dark. She sat up, wiping her mouth with the back of her sleeve and prayed that she hadn't been snoring as well.

Still raining.

She looked out of the windscreen at the little darts of water shining in the headlights. Everything beyond them was so black. There were no street lamps. The road was narrow, hemmed in on either side by tall hedges which loomed in the light from the car. Ghostly wisps of mist swam in the road ahead of them. The radio was off: the only sound now came from the engine and the wipers, swiping at the rain.

'Have a good sleep?' Tristan asked softly.

'Yeah. Thanks,' Summer mumbled. She rubbed her eyes. They felt as though they were coated in sand. Her tongue was furry. She ran it across her teeth.

Rank.

'Nearly there. Rain's come on harder.'

Summer said nothing.

'I can fix you a hot drink once we get in; a snack, if you like?'

He was trying too hard.

'I'm fine,' she mumbled.

'Or you can just go straight to bed. I'll make you a hot-water bottle.' He let out a nervy chuckle. 'Hot-water bottles in July – crazy! But you'll see, the house can get quite cold. It's an old place. Gets damp, you know.'

No, I don't know.

Even as she wished he would shut up, she felt a stab of guilt. He was only trying to be friendly. She was wasting this time with him, being so sullen. She should be using the journey to ask him things, to prepare herself.

She opened her mouth to form a question.

'Here we are!' Tristan announced. The car turned sharply to the left and two great stone pillars came into view. 'Welcome to Bosleven,' he said with a note of pride.

Passing between the pillars, the car continued down an even darker, narrower road. The headlights revealed huge bushes of nodding, phantom-pale flowers lining the way.

'The hydrangeas. Welcoming us home,' he said.

'What?'

'Those bushes.' Tristan nodded towards the windscreen.

Summer peered out at the blossomy heads, knocking together in the rain, smashing against the side of the car.

'Hydrangeas,' he repeated. 'You'll see them

24

everywhere. They like the warm climate.'

Summer was confused. 'You said we'd arrived.'

'We have.'

'So why are we still going, then?' she said.

'Oh, this is the drive. Not far now.'

Not far now, not far.

He kept saying that. The house must be enormous to have such a grand entrance. Why would her mother send her to a massive house down a dark lane at the far end of the country? Summer's skin crawled. Right now, all she could think was that she was an orphan, sent away to live with a strange uncle in a scary big house. Like Mary Lennox in *The Secret Garden*, she thought, with a touch of drama.

She rubbed briskly at her arms and sat up straight.

You're being ridiculous.

Then the house was in front of them; a small light on outside the porch, trees swaying; the facade of the building, imposing, tall and dark.

She got out of the car. Her trainers crunched on gravel underfoot. She pulled her thin jacket tightly around her. The rain lashed her hair across her face.

Not a 'barbecue summer' down here then.

'Come on, let's get you inside quickly,' Tristan urged.

He battled with the front door, wiggling a key in the lock and muttering under his breath. An owl called, high and desolate. Summer jumped, then, embarrassed, glanced at Tristan to see if he had noticed, but he was still engaged in his battle with the door. It cooperated abruptly without warning, opening inwards. Tristan lunged forward.

He recovered his footing, muttering apologies, and flicked a switch. Pale light fell in a pool on the floor, bringing to faded life the dimly lit features of a large hallway. A grandfather clock stood against the wall to the right, aloof and dark.

'Two o'clock already!' Summer exclaimed, peering at the hands on the worn, dirty face.

Tristan turned and smiled. 'No, no. That old thing hasn't worked for years. It's half past midnight – give or take,' he said, checking his watch. 'Come into the kitchen. I'll put the kettle on.'

'No, it's OK. I'd – I'd rather go straight to bed. Please,' she added.

A look of concern flickered across her uncle's face.

'Of course.' He took off his raincoat and hung it on a wrought-iron coat stand, overloaded with other coats, jackets, hats and umbrellas. 'I will make you a hot-water bottle though – I'm going to have one! Do take your jacket off. You must be soaked.' He continued talking about the rain and how he was sure it would be gone by the morning while he bustled into the kitchen to make the hot-water bottles.

Summer hung her jacket on top of the other

paraphernalia on the coat stand. She did not know whether to follow Tristan or not. She did not want to encourage him to make any more conversation or press her to have a hot chocolate, so she decided to stay where she was, waiting, as she tried to focus her tired eyes.

She wanted to take in every detail of the hallway, but it was so big, and still gloomy, even with the light on. Shadows flickered in the corners; the ceiling went on forever; the floor was tiled, black-and-white; everything looked ancient. There was wood panelling on the walls up to waist height and ahead of her an imposing, winding wooden staircase which spiralled up into the pitch blackness of the floor above. It was a house straight out of a fairy tale, and not a good one: one about a stranger luring a girl into a house and then . . .

Panic crawled over her skin.

I don't want to be here, I don't want to be here, I don't want to be here.

She had the same sudden urge to turn and run that she had felt in the station and had to grip the side of a shelf by the door to steady herself. She made herself look at the shelf, talk herself through what was on it: a bowl of keys, some large, rubbery green gloves, a golf ball, a table tennis bat with chewed edges.

'Oh!' She started as she saw, out of the corner of her eye, something white skitter up the stairs.

'There you are.' Tristan had come back with the hot-water bottles. 'Sorry, did I make you jump? You do look pale. I'm sorry, I shouldn't witter on. Straight to your room, yes?'

Summer nodded, tried to calm herself.

What was that thing? A mouse? Maybe they have a cat.

Tristan had already turned to the stairs. He flicked another switch, this time to turn on the wall lights, and beckoned to her to follow him up the staircase. There was a half-landing with rooms off it, then the staircase turned, leading to a longer corridor with more rooms and a bookcase at the end. There were stairs to the left leading up to another floor.

The house was vast! Completely silent too. Summer picked up a faint damp smell and felt the walls close in around her. The light from the wall lamps was as dim as that in the hall, so that when a white shape darted across the floor of the landing in front of them, Summer gave a gasp and stumbled.

Tristan stopped. 'All right?'

It was a cat. Get a grip, Summer.

'Yeah, I'm – I'm fine. Just tripped over the—'

'Oh, the carpet!' Tristan exclaimed. He pointed down sheepishly at Summer's foot which had got caught in a hole in the frayed Persian runner. 'Sorry about that. It's very old,' he said.

'No worries.' Summer pulled her foot out of the ragged hole.

'OK.' Tristan gestured ahead to the right. 'Your room's just along here.'

'Next to the bookcase at the end?' Summer asked, pointing to the end of the corridor.

'Yes. Your room's just above the old kitchen passage, where the servants worked – years and years ago, I mean. No servants now, more's the pity.' He was trying to keep his voice light and jokey. 'You can access it from the hall – Kenan will show you tomorrow. The attic's above you. Nothing to show you there – just boxes of junk.'

Attic? Kitchen passage? Servants?

What *was* this place?

Tristan saw the look of confusion on her face. 'Don't worry. I know the house seems enormous, but it's really not as muddling as it seems. You will have a proper tour tomorrow.'

Summer could not help smirking at that. A tour of her old home in London would have taken all of five minutes: lounge, two tiny bedrooms, kitchen, shower, loo. Done.

They walked along the landing and stopped by the bookcase. Summer glanced at the books. The spines looked ancient: broken, dusty with gold embossed lettering.

'I hope you like it,' Tristan pushed open the door, pulled a cord hanging to the left and showed her the illuminated room with a flourish.

She had been determined not to be impressed, to hate what she was shown, to reject everything offered, but the room was beautiful. She imagined standing in her own home (her *old* home, she corrected herself), saw this bedroom land on top of it, swallowing it up in one gulp. The ceiling soared, the curtains were floor-length, made of some heavy, faded red fabric with tassels on the ends. As for the heavy wooden wardrobe and chest of drawers, they were surely antique. The very air in the room seemed antique; thin, as though it had been breathed a million times before over hundreds and hundreds of years.

I could reach out and touch the past.

And the bed!

It was a four-poster, high off the ground, set against the middle of the wall and filling a good portion of the room.

The Princess and the Pea! Proper Fairy Land now.

Tristan chuckled. 'Bit over the top, I know. Hope you don't mind. It's been in the family for a while.'

Unlike me.

'Yeah, it's – cool,' she managed, blushing.

'So I'll leave you to it – oh, and the bathroom's opposite, across the landing. It's all yours: ours is on the half-landing, next to my room. No one'll disturb you. Sleep as long as you like. As I say, Kenan will, no doubt! I won't clear breakfast away until you're down, so there's no hurry in the morning. Night, then.' He handed her one of the hot-water bottles, gave a small smile and closed the door softly behind him.

Summer held her breath, waited until his footsteps had receded, then hurriedly plonked the hot-water bottle on the bed, pulled her T-shirt and pyjama bottoms from the top of a case and changed. She tiptoed out on to the dimly lit landing and saw Tristan had turned on the light in the bathroom opposite.

He is trying to make me feel welcome.

Tiredness weighed heavily on her now. She fumbled her way through cleaning her teeth and using the lavatory before climbing up into the regal bed. There was a dip in the mattress which seemed to fit her body perfectly. She curled into a ball and held the hot-water bottle, cuddling it close, grateful for its comfort and warmth.

Kind. He is kind.

She was dimly aware of feeling suddenly completely safe. She tried to work out why this was, to catch hold of a thought swimming through her mind, but it slipped out of reach and became blurred before disappearing under the warmth of the bedclothes and a tidal wave of exhaustion.

Chapter Four

Summer stirred and mumbled in protest as light filtered through her dream-heavy eyelashes. She turned to look at her watch where she had left it on the table next to her.

Quarter to eleven – not a bad lie-in.

Her mind snapped to attention as she remembered where she was. The questions she had wanted to ask Tristan the night before jostled and nagged. Why had her mum sent her here? Why had she thought this was a good place for her to be? Why had she never mentioned or discussed it? Tristan had seemed to take it all in his stride. How could he be so accepting? Had he known about her for much longer than he was letting on? What about his wife?

The questions ricocheted, making her heart pound.

Then she heard her mother's voice, so clearly, it was as though she were right beside her: 'Bye, love.'

Summer pulled the sheets up over her head, her jaw tight.

No, no more tears. Can't go down and face him if I start blubbing again.

She was about to get up when she heard a scuffle of footsteps and a voice, very close, outside the door.

'Kenan! Come away! Leave her be. We didn't get home until gone midnight.'

Tristan's voice, reprimanding. Then a grumbling younger voice.

Summer stayed stock-still and listened. There were footsteps again, retreating this time, and then silence.

Once she was sure they had gone, she breathed again, jumped out of bed and went to the thick red curtains. She was both curious and fearful to see what might be beyond the high-ceilinged, echoey room.

She took hold of the edge of a curtain in each hand and threw them back hastily, as though ripping off a plaster on a grazed knee. As the wooden curtain rings rattled across the rail it occurred to her that she might be on the point of giving the world a view of her tatty nightclothes. At home the bedroom window looked out on to the street. The block of flats had been close enough to the pavement that people could look in if they had nothing better to do.

She need not have worried. As she focused on the scene before her, she saw that whatever else was going to happen from now on, one thing was certain: the only spying from outside would be done by tall pine trees, glowing in golden sunlight, swaying in a light breeze.

There was not one single house to be seen, only lawns, trees, and in the distance, the sea.

Summer had never felt more alone.

The bathroom was white: white walls, white bath, white loo.

Summer bent over to free the bath plug from its coil around the taps, but leaped back in alarm, a scream catching in her throat.

An enormous brown-black spider with eyes out on stalks was skulking near the plughole. She brushed at it with fearful stabbing motions until it gave up all hope of peace and quiet and reluctantly scuttled down the hole. Summer hastily blocked its escape route with the plug and fumbled with the taps. The water blasted out in a torrent of heat and steam, causing her to jump again.

Owls. Cats. Giant spiders. Boiling bath water . . .

Would her heart ever settle back to its normal rhythm? It didn't help that she felt she was being watched. She was sure she heard scuffling noises outside the door. Was Kenan spying on her again?

She crept over while the water was running and put her eye to the keyhole. There was no one on the landing. Just in case, she put the key in the lock and turned it firmly, hearing the reassuring *clunk* of the heavy metal bolt sliding home.

More noises; this time from beneath her feet.

Maybe there are mice under the floorboards?

She reminded herself there was a cat in the house. It would deal with any mice.

The bath was deep and the warm water gave off a honey-sweet aroma as the steam rose and clouded the room. Summer sank into it, feeling the tension rolling off her shoulders. She looked up at the ceiling and watched the watery patterns reflected there.

Her moment of peace was shattered by someone throwing something at the door. She sat up abruptly, sloshing water on to the floor tiles.

'When are you going to show your face then?' said a voice. It was low, menacing, or so it seemed to Summer, who slid quickly down below the rim of the bath in case the key was not enough of a screen against a spy.

It was him. Kenan.

'I – I'm in the bath,' she called out.

Of course I'm in the flipping bath, I'm not snorkelling in here, am I?

She heard him run away, sniggering.

Summer scrambled out, dried herself hurriedly. She didn't want to be here, but she couldn't hide forever, and even if she did, would he be outside every door, snooping? She decided not to give him another chance.

At least he wasn't waiting for her once she had finished in the bathroom and got dressed. Now that she was on the landing, Summer could not hear any more noises, not even the scuttling under the floorboards. The house no longer seemed as forbidding as it had in the dark the night before. The walls on the stairway and in the hall were painted a soft, comforting terracotta and were bathed in light which flooded in through the windows and glass of the front door.

Warm and welcoming.

She told herself to think positive. At least in a house this size she would not be in the family's pockets. If she and her cousin did not hit it off, they could give each other space. That was good. And there would be something to do today: she could explore. Judging by the view from her window, there was a lot of exploring to do, outside as well as in.

Mum wanted me to live here. So she must have known the place – loved it, I guess.

Summer decided she needed to try to see Bosleven through her mother's eyes. She squared her shoulders and headed for the kitchen, where she could hear a low murmuring conversation, the words too softly spoken to reach her ears.

As she stepped into the hallway, the door to the kitchen opened slightly and the white cat slipped out. The animal stopped, fixed her with an appraising stare, then yawned abruptly, flicked its tail and was gone.

Such blue eyes! Must ask what it's called . . .

Summer went into the room. Tristan was sitting at the kitchen table which was set against a large, high window overlooking the garden. He rose, smiling uncertainly, as she entered the room, his chair scraping on the wooden floor. One other face was turned up to look at hers, unsmiling. Hostile, even.

Summer automatically took a step back.

'Summer,' Tristan said, announcing her presence in the same way he had at the station. Summer felt he might just as well have said, 'At last.'

'I – I'm sorry I slept in,' she muttered, lowering her eyes. She wished the boy would say something, not simply glare at her.

'Nonsense,' said Tristan, his smile spreading, reaching his eyes. They were very dark; the pupils merged into the inky irises. 'You needed a good sleep,' he added.

'Yes,' she said. 'I was – I am tired.'

She wanted so much to look at these people and find a connection, a family likeness, something to reassure her. How well had they known her mother? Were they sad about her death? Maybe they felt nothing. Maybe she, Summer, was nothing to them either.

She swallowed, gave her head the tiniest of shakes.

Mustn't . . .

'Come and say hello.' Tristan was holding out a hand as though to encourage her. 'Have some breakfast. You must be starving. You didn't have anything last night.

We're on our second breakfast already, aren't we?' he joked, nodding to the boy, who continued to stare brazenly.

Summer approached the table. Piles of paper and recently opened post were heaped at one end. Three places were set at the other, Tristan's chair at the head, the boy's so that he sat with his back to the large window. Summer was offered a place opposite him.

'So. This is Kenan,' Tristan spoke into the awkward silence. 'Your – cousin,' he added, reddening.

The boy let out a derisive snort, but was quickly silenced by a look from his father.

'And, er, Becca – my wife – she's not joining us just now,' he said, his smile quivering slightly.

'Not *ever* at this rate,' Kenan retorted. His voice had a raw edge, wavering uncertainly between that of a boy and a man.

Tristan raised his eyebrows pointedly at his son.

'Yeah, whatever,' Kenan sneered, then, to Summer: 'Hi, *cousin*. Toast or cereal?' He made it sound as though he was offering the choice between being shot or hanged.

'I – oh, cereal's fine.'

Summer took the chair offered her by her uncle and accepted a glass of juice and bowl of muesli with a subdued 'Thank you'.

Silence seeped back into the room, reproachful,

suspicious. Summer wished that the old grandfather clock worked so that there would at least be a solid, reassuring, ticking sound to listen to as she slowly chewed the oaty chunks of cereal. She thought of how Mum would have been at breakfast if they had a guest – like when Jess stayed over. Music would be playing, the window open in weather like this. Mum would be laughing, singing, offering to make pancakes. Jess and she would be noisy. The house would roar with life.

Tristan spoke into the heavy atmosphere with laboured cheerfulness. 'I was thinking you could take Summer for a little tour today, Kenan,' he said. 'Show her the farm, the rockery – I'm sure she'd like to see the beach.'

'No way!' Kenan spluttered through a mouthful of cereal.

'Kenan!' Tristan objected. 'Summer has come a long way. She has gone through a lot recently. Remember what I told you.'

'It's OK,' Summer said. 'I don't need looking after.'

Not by you.

'There, see?' the boy spat. 'She doesn't need me. I'm getting the bus into town today in any case.'

'It wouldn't do you any harm . . .'

Summer focused on working her way through her breakfast. She didn't feel at all hungry. All she wanted was to get out of that room. Suddenly the prospect of exploring the house did not seem so appealing.

39

Kenan pushed his chair back and left the table. He took his breakfast things over to the dishwasher and yanked the machine open, rattling the contents as he crammed his stuff in.

'I'm sorry,' Tristan said. 'We – this is an adjustment for us too. I don't mean to sound unkind, but it was a bit of a shock. I didn't know Cat— didn't know your mum was . . .' He stopped himself and turned his face away.

'You could have said no,' Kenan barked.

'Kenan!' Tristan turned back to face his son, distraught at the boy's behaviour.

Kenan's face was hard, but he said no more. Another heavy curtain of silence fell.

He is angry. Of course he is. Why should *he want me here?*

Summer tried to imagine how she would be if her mum had told her one day that another child, a stranger, would be coming to live with them. She knew her mother would be gentle in her persuasion that it was the right thing to do. It would be a decision they made together. Her mother would not impose something this big on her unless it was hugely important, and Summer would understand that. She and her mother had never spoken to each other in the harsh tone Kenan was using. They had disagreed, Summer had moaned about things, said things weren't fair. Somehow, though, being just the two of them, they had been a team. But she knew that no two

40

families worked the same way. She would have to find out how this one operated.

Other people's houses. Other people's rules.

With some obvious effort, Tristan resumed a more reasonable tone. 'Kenan, will you please put off your plans to go into town and show Summer around. I have some work to do until lunchtime, then I'll run you both in later if you like. Save you the bus fare.'

'Looks like I don't have a choice,' Kenan muttered.

It was going to take some doing to get to know this boy, Summer thought. But she would have to.

Neither of them had a choice.

Chapter Five

Summer followed Kenan out of the kitchen. He waited until they were out of earshot, then he hissed, 'Just so you know, I am doing this for Dad.'

'Just so you know, so am I,' Summer snapped back.

Not going to let him think I'm a walkover.

Her retort clearly took him by surprise. His eyes widened for a second. 'Fine.'

He turned his back to the kitchen door and made for a corridor Summer had not noticed in the dark the night before.

'Where are you going?'

'What do you mean, where am I going? I'm showing you around, aren't I? Coming, or what?'

Summer frowned and glanced at the front door.

Kenan gave a snort of laughter. 'We don't go out *that* way unless we're taking the car.' He said it as though she were dense not to realize how and when the front door was used. She would not have been surprised if he had started talking about there being a 'tradesmen's entrance'.

'So where *are* we going? Aren't you going to show me the house?'

His narrow eyes glinted. 'Why? Planning on ripping us off, are you?'

'What?'

'Just stop asking so many questions and follow me.' He had already turned away and set off down the corridor at a pace.

I haven't even started with the questions yet, mate.

Light filled the passage, which was airier than the panelled hallway. She looked up to see skylights in the ceiling, far out of reach, coated in cobwebs on the inside, birds' droppings on the outside. She pictured Tristan using a long brush or feather duster to clean it, his arms at full stretch, reaching into the corners.

There was a clattering noise from the other side of the right-hand wall.

'What was that?' she asked, before she could stop herself.

But Kenan did not seem to have heard.

'This is the kitchen passage,' he was saying in a bored voice. 'Used to be where the *servants* worked,' he added, looking at her pointedly.

'Yeah, your dad said. So tell me about these servants then?'

I have soooo much in common with these people . . .

Kenan rolled his eyes. 'There aren't any *now*. God,

43

Mum would *kill* for a couple of servants. Running this place is hard work.'

My heart bleeds . . .

'The old kitchen was down here, but we don't use it now. These rooms are all storage,' Kenan continued, waving vaguely at doors to the left. 'Then there's the—' He stopped abruptly, seeming to have changed his mind about something. 'Yeah, anyway, you don't really need to know about this,' he went on hastily. 'Like I say, we don't use it.'

Summer frowned. 'Bit of a waste of space, all this?' she said.

'Well, not that it's any of your business, but this part used to be for holiday lets,' Kenan muttered.

Summer shrugged. The mood the boy was in, this could turn out to be a long morning. She made a show of looking into the rooms on the left as they passed them so that she could avoid any further conversation. They were rammed with jumbled items. Large green shutters kept out the light, so that it was hard to discern the objects. She thought she saw a bike, some old furniture, paint pots, ladders, an ironing board. The right-hand side of the passage was smooth, red wall; no doors, apart from one ahead of them at the end.

'Locked,' Kenan muttered, when he saw her looking. 'Like I said, it's just storage. Junk rooms.'

Summer made a face. 'Whatever.'

There was a faint, pleasantly briny smell and a damp chill in the air. The smell of the place and the reddish-brown paint brought to mind a small villa that a friend of her mother's had lent them a couple of years back. A holiday abroad. A rare treat. The thick stone walls had provided a soothing, cool fortress from the Mediterranean furnace-blast that hit them whenever they had ventured out in the middle of the day.

A sudden noise brought her out of her reverie. It was coming from beyond the wall to her right.

'Are there more rooms on the other side?' she asked, pointing in the direction of the sound. It was as if someone were moving furniture around, dragging something heavy across the floor.

Kenan's face darkened. 'Listen, this is my house. I'm the one showing *you* around, OK?' he snapped.

'Hey, chill! I was only asking—'

'Yeah, well don't. I've already told you. We keep stuff in there and it's locked. So don't go getting any ideas!'

Summer's jaw tightened.

I swear I'm going to hit him if he carries on like this.

Kenan must have realized he had gone too far, for his eyes softened and he seemed to make an effort to relax. 'There's a table-tennis table in here,' he said, gesturing casually to the last room on the left.

She ignored him, straining to catch the sounds from beyond the wall again, but they had stopped.

'Do you play?' Kenan persisted.

'Maybe.'

'Well . . . I could teach you,' he said.

Don't force yourself.

'Yeah.'

'No big deal.' Kenan turned and walked away.

She immediately felt bad: it would have cost him, offering to play with her like that. She sighed as she looked in at the table-tennis table – which had more paint pots heaped on top of it.

No one's played with him for a while, then.

'So do you play with your dad – or mum?' Summer asked.

But Kenan was striding ahead now. The moment of tentative friendliness had passed as quickly as it had come.

Somehow, Summer could not see Tristan taking the time to play table tennis with Kenan: the way the father and son had been with each other earlier – she could not envisage matey afternoons spent playing and joking together.

Maybe that's what's made him so grumpy – nothing to do with me at all.

They had come to the end of the corridor. Kenan was leaning with his back against another door, pushing it open. A narrow beam of sunlight crept in and lit up the tiles on the floor. 'This leads to the garden.

Mum's pride and joy,' he was saying.

Summer felt a trickle of cold run down her back as he said this. She was suddenly convinced that they were not alone. She glanced behind her.

Someone is *watching me.*

Somewhere a door banged. Summer's heart caught in her throat.

Kenan did not seem to have noticed anything. 'Your room's above here. As it's above the kitchen passage, the servants probably slept in *your* bit.' He grinned.

This idea seemed to please him, that she should be put away in the servants' quarters. Before she could think of a suitable retort, Kenan leaned towards her and rasped: 'This part of the house is haunted.' He opened his eyes wide to make his point. 'Especially up where *you* are! Must be the old servants, rattling around in the woodwork.' He whirled away from her again and gave the door a shove, dancing jauntily through and waving his arms in a ghostly fashion, calling, 'Whoooo! Whoooo!'

'Yeah, right!' said Summer. 'So how come there are no ghosts in the main part of the house, then?' Her voice bounced shrilly off the damp walls, betraying her fear.

Kenan glanced back at her, that stupid grin on his face again. 'How should I know? Maybe the servants were particularly *bad* while they were alive,' he said. 'And now they just can't rest in peace.'

He was a jerk, talking about death like that. He knew

47

about her mum. What did he think he would achieve by trying to spook her? She could not run away. She was here for good now, whether he wanted it or not.

She felt something snap inside her.

'Why are you being such a—?'

He squared up to her. 'What?'

'I mean what have I *done* to you? I've only been here five minutes – and it's not like it's out of choice – and you're . . . you're behaving like I'm here specifically to make your life hell!' She shook her head. 'If it makes you feel any better, I didn't want to come here.'

'No. It doesn't make me feel better,' Kenan countered. Without waiting for a reaction, he turned away again and scurried down some stone steps and on to a cobbled walkway, lined by imposing grey walls.

No choice but to follow.

They went through a wrought-iron gate and out into a gravel-coated area with a formal flower bed. The air was sweet with last night's rain, the walls reflected heat and light from the startlingly golden sun. The warmth was a welcome surprise after the cold of the house.

Summer looked up and drank in the deep blue of the sky, the small smudges of white cloud. Something swooped low over her head and curved up sharply in front of her, making her duck.

'Swallows,' Kenan said. 'Not seen them before?' he added, seeing the look on her face. 'They nest here every year.' He turned left and had his hand on the latch of a sage-green wooden door in the wall. 'Their favourite places are in the eaves and in the woodshed.' He spoke with pride.

He's loving this, playing Lord of the Manor.

'Right,' Summer said. She refused to sound impressed.

She looked up and saw the little nests snug under the rafters of the house.

Maybe that's what's making those scuffling noises.

A fleeting image passed through her mind of the dusty London pigeons sheltering under the arches near the station back home.

Another world.

The swallows zipped in and out of the covered passage she had just walked through. Tiny faces with wide-stretched beaks appeared at the edge of the nest. Chicks set up a clamouring, their scrawny heads reaching towards the adult bird approaching, desperate to be the first to be fed. The parent hovered expertly, popping morsels into the hungry mouths before flitting off again to fetch more food.

What would happen to them if the adult failed to show one day? No guardian would swoop in and take them under its wing. They would be left to fend for themselves, or to perish.

So what made her more important than one of these chicks, that she should be swept up and cared for by

Kenan and his family? They had had a life without her. A simpler life.

She was unwanted baggage. A nuisance that had to be accommodated.

She glanced at Kenan.

Survival of the fittest. Which of us would it be?

'You coming or what?' Kenan said, breaking into her thoughts. 'Walled garden,' he said, as he opened the door and went in.

Summer hesitated.

'So?'

'Yeah, yeah. Coming.' She felt her throat tighten. If her mother had been here, she would have walked through this very door, seen what she, Summer, was now seeing.

Did you live here, Mum? A long time ago?

She felt something soft brush her ankle and looked down to see the little white cat, winding its way in and out of her legs, purring loudly. She bent to pick it up, wanting to hold it to her, to feel her arms around something. But the cat slithered out of her grasp with a soft mew and ran back to the house.

Why didn't she tell me about this place? It's obvious it's pretty special. Why keep it a secret?

'As I said, Mum's pride and joy.' Kenan stepped aside and gestured as though he had conjured up the scene before them.

'Oh!'

Kenan blushed when he saw Summer was wide-eyed. 'Cool, isn't it?'

Summer nodded. She saw he had let his guard slip, letting her catch a glimpse of what the place meant to him.

No wonder he was chuffed, she thought, gazing around. This was *The Secret Garden* after all, and she *was* Mary Lennox!

Can't see Kenan as Dickon, though; for all his chit-chat about the swallows.

There were four separate sections to the garden: one a neat vegetable patch, one a miniature maze, another with an umbrella-like tree in the middle, and the fourth planted artfully with pink and purple flowers. Gravel paths acted as dividers and in the very centre of the garden was a pond with a fountain.

'It's amazing,' Summer breathed.

So perfect, so still and quiet: Summer felt she was spying on a private world that rarely invited, or welcomed, visitors.

'Isn't it? Mum's own design,' Kenan said, that edge of pride in his voice again.

Seeing the carefully planted garden, so neat and tidy, Summer knew then, without a doubt.

This is Mum all over.

Her mother had loved gardens, always been wistful

about what she would do if she had had the space. Tears welled up in Summer as she saw in her mind's eye the rows of pots on their small London patio, the sweet peas growing up the trellis.

She was here, then. Had to be.

Kenan was looking at her strangely. She swallowed, forced herself to say something. 'She must be clever. Your mum.'

'She is.' A cloud passed over his features. He looked lost; younger suddenly.

'Are you—?' Summer wanted to ask him if he was all right, but she did not trust her voice.

She turned away to the pond, blinking hard, and forced herself to focus on the huge orange-and-white fish which rose up through the murky green depths.

'I bet the cat has a go at these,' she called. A change of subject to lighten the atmosphere.

He frowned. 'What?'

She opened her mouth to repeat herself. Kenan had already turned swiftly away, however, and was walking back out of the garden, as though regretting ever showing her the place.

'Let's go,' he shouted, when she did not make a move to follow.

'OK! OK! What's the rush?' She jogged over to catch up with him. 'Will I meet your mum later?' she added.

'How do I know?' Kenan would not look at her.

'Tell me what's going on. Please?' she said. Then, more quietly, 'Has she – is she cross or something? Because of me?'

Kenan continued to ignore her, walking fast, head down, brows knitted together.

'Kenan?' she tried again. 'Something's upset you. What is it?'

'Dad says I have to show you round, and that's what I'm doing, OK?' he said irritably. 'So either follow me or go and find something else to do.'

And what would that be exactly?

Yet again, she did not have a choice.

Kenan's dark mood did not lift as he marched Summer around the sprawling grounds. He carried out a sullen, bored inventory, pointing out where the sea was, explaining that the 'side walk' (a path that ran along the far edge of the lawn) had once been the main driveway to the house.

'So how come it was changed then?' Summer asked.

This at last seemed to provoke something in the boy. He stopped and she saw that expression of wicked amusement flicker across his face again.

'Because of the ghosts.'

Summer rolled her eyes. 'Ghosts in the house, ghosts in the garden. You don't give up, do you?'

'It's true,' he insisted, suddenly animated. 'When

people used horses and carriages, the horses used to come down that way and they would always get spooked at the same point. It got to the stage people didn't want to come and visit any more, so the owners made the driveway we use today.' He nodded in the direction of the drive she had come down the previous night. 'Come on, I'll show you where the ghosts are.'

He strode ahead, his long legs carrying him quickly across the lawn. She saw the shadow of his father in the way he moved. Kenan had the same rangy body, the same thick, dark messy hair.

She hesitated as he headed for the path, partly concealed behind shrubbery, trees and more of those large blue-flowered bushes Tristan had showed her the night before. What had he called them? High-something. They bent their blowsy heads low, casting cool shady shapes over the path.

'Come on!' He was urging her to follow.

Don't be a wimp. He wants *you to think spooky thoughts. You don't believe in ghosts.*

Didn't she? What about that unexplained phone call the night her mother died?

She felt goosebumps rise on her arms, in spite of the warmth from the sun.

'Wait, can't you?'

She ran into the shadows to catch up.

Kenan was standing in a sun-dappled spot on the

dirt-track. 'It's here!' he said. 'This is the place.' His thin pale face was flushed with excitement, a little boy again, enjoying his story, as though caught up in an adventure.

He's playing make-believe.

'How do you know this is it?' Summer looked around, sceptically. 'It's never wide enough here for a horse and carriage.'

Kenan would not be put off. 'I told you, they changed it. After the horses got spooked so many times. By the ghost. It definitely feels colder here than anywhere else in the garden. That's what they say about ghosts, isn't it? That you feel a chill if there's one about? What d'you reckon?'

She thought of the chill she herself had felt in the old kitchen passage when she had been certain someone was watching her. Maybe he wasn't trying to scare her: he seemed genuinely to believe what he was saying and to want her approval, for her to share something with him.

She couldn't let him have the satisfaction, though. Her mouth twisted. 'Oh, come on. You don't really believe that rubbish?'

Kenan's bright-eyed expression vanished. 'Whatever,' he said. Then, drawing himself up, 'Since you obviously know everything, you don't need me, so you can piss off now.'

'What?'

'You heard me. Piss off. I didn't have to show you

round. It's not like I haven't got other things to do.'

She held up a hand to pacify him. 'Hey, I only meant . . . No need to be so—' she began.

Kenan had broken into a run, was sprinting across the lawn towards the house.

A lump rose in her throat. She hadn't exactly been enjoying his company, but . . . she didn't much want to be left alone like this either.

What am I going to do now?

She felt guilty. Kenan had been upset in the walled garden; something to do with when she had asked about his mother. She should have been nicer to him. She was the stranger, this was his home. But . . . oh! She needed someone to take care of her too.

She looked towards the house again. He had definitely tried to put the wind up her with all his talk about hauntings. That wasn't kind, was it, whatever he was feeling? It was hardly subtle either, bringing up the subject of ghosts when he knew her mother had died so recently.

Ghosts.

She shuddered, but not because she was standing in the leafy shade. It was a sudden, iron chill that clutched at her heart.

Because there, on the far side of the garden, staring out at her from the darkened porch at the front of the house, was her mother.

Chapter Six

'Mum?'

Summer was running, her feet pounding the grass, her legs not moving fast enough, as though pushing through deep, cold water.

'MUM!'

When she reached the porch, there was nothing there. No one. She was sobbing; her chest heaving. She took hold of the front-door knob and wrenched it this way and that, rattled it ferociously.

Locked.

What is happening to me? First that phone call and now this. I don't believe in this stuff. It's all his fault.

She let her hands fall to her sides and stood weeping.

What are you doing? *She is not here. She is not anywhere.*

Summer shook her head, trying to push the tears away, and to rid her mind of the sight of her mother in the porch, looking right at her.

She rubbed her nose hard on the back of her hand, blinked angrily. She could not bear the thought of Kenan watching her from inside the house, and knew that she could not go back in. She could not face Kenan or Tristan. She turned and looked back at the path.

There must be a way out of this place. The sea was that way, he said.

She was not thinking clearly now, only knew how she felt – hemmed in, spied on. By whom? By Kenan, hiding somewhere in the house? Or by someone or something more unsettling?

She pushed that thought away as she ran back to the shady path, looking about her wildly. If this was the old drive, then a right turn would take her back to the road Tristan had driven them along the previous night.

So left to the sea then.

Even though she could not know where she was going, Summer did not question the decision she had made. She did not want to stop and think. Stopping and thinking seemed only to lead to unwanted memories, tears, and visions of things she would rather not see. So she pushed forward beneath the green and brown canopy, ran through the shadows and beams of light, and away from the house.

There! A five-bar gate ahead. She wrestled with the catch and was out, on a track that sloped down to the right, away from the house, with open fields on both sides.

She gazed along the track.

To the sea.

She ran on, sweating, wishing she had worn shorts instead of jeans. Her armpits were damp and uncomfortable, her feet rubbed painfully in her trainers. She could have walked, of course she could. But what if Kenan or Tristan decided to come looking for her? No, she needed to get away quickly; needed space.

Another gate.

She heard Tristan's voice echoing in her head: 'Show her the farm, the rockery . . . the beach.'

Did he own the farm? Or would she find herself wandering on to someone else's property? She looked at the gate. No 'Private' signs. She swallowed, checked about her, then pushed the gate open and ran through. A path swept away and down, lined thickly on either side with more and more of those big blue flowers they had back at the house.

The bushes towered over her, the great floppy heads heavy with moisture from last night's rainfall. As she brushed past them, droplets of water fell on to her T-shirt, running in rivulets down her arms, cooling her skin. She couldn't see where the path was heading and began to feel a little foolish.

Maybe I should turn back. What am I going to do when I get . . . wherever I'm going?

She gave one final push against the greenery; the leaves parted like curtains and the path ran out. A deep bowl of riotous colour fell away beneath her: cascading ferns; huge balls of tiny, purple-indigo flowers; dragon-tongued fronds of red and orange; trumpets of white. And among them a stream, pure and fresh, trickling down over moss-streaked rocks. Around this paradise rose giant granite boulders, the crevices in them like features on ancient faces, looking down on the place, protecting it.

From people like me.

Summer felt sure she should not be in this beautiful garden. It was too special, too private. Or maybe . . . was this the rockery?

A rockery – that's a garden with rocks in, right?

Well, this was a garden, and there were loads of rocks in it. But 'rockery' did not really cover it – the place was more like something out of *Alice's Adventures in Wonderland*. Those huge leaves, like giant versions of the rhubarb plants her mother had grown in pots on the balcony: looking up at them made her feel as though she were shrinking.

More fairy-tale stuff.

Still, if this was the rockery, it must be part of Bosleven, so presumably it was fine to be here.

That was a lot to assume, though. She felt a strong sense that she was not supposed to be here; that *any* human would feel unwelcome here. The garden had the air of a lost world about it. Lost or forgotten.

She dropped her eyes to the leaf-strewn, mossy ground and tried to concentrate, to make a plan. She listened to the gentle lapping of the water at her feet and thought of what she knew about streams and rivers.

'Streams flow to the sea.' So I'll follow this stream. Maybe it will take me to the beach.

She did not move on right away. Maybe she should turn back.

She wavered, was about to retrace her steps, when . . .

'Miaaaow!'

'Oh, hello! You again.' Summer crouched low to stroke the little white cat.

The cat tilted its heart-shaped face up to hers, closed its eyes and seemed almost to smile as it rubbed its head against her knees and let forth a deep, jet-engine purr. It had a silvery-grey collar that she hadn't noticed before, a small name tag dangling from it.

'Let's have a look . . . What's your name, eh?' she caught hold of the metal disc and turned it over. Only the letter 'C' was visible, the rest of the name rubbed out, the metal smooth.

'Well, "C", maybe you can answer another question,' Summer said, letting go of the disc. 'Is this garden part of Bosleven? Or are you trespassing too?'

The cat sat back on its haunches and washed one paw thoughtfully. Then it fixed her with its cool blue eyes and said, *'Miaoooow!'*

'Really?' said Summer. 'Don't suppose you know the way to the beach as well?'

The cat flattened its ears, hissed, and darted away, down the path alongside the stream.

Summer straightened up, shook her head.

Talking to a cat now. Bonkers.

She followed it, all the same.

The stream was shallow and the rocks acted as stepping stones. As she passed by the granite faces, she avoided their stony gaze.

Don't be stupid. They're just lumps of rock.

The cat bounded ahead, stopping every so often as though checking that Summer was keeping up.

The stream ran on through a thicket lined with rocks and old tree stumps standing silent and watchful.

Summer glanced over her shoulder as she followed the white cat.

Still alone.

The woodland gave way to denser undergrowth. Brambles and nettles had won over this territory. Summer was grateful for her jeans now and wished she had long sleeves too.

The brambles tore at her bare skin, her hair was caught and tangled on thorns, but she pushed on. The roar of the sea was filling her ears already, its salty tang in her nostrils. She leaned into the branches that stubbornly blocked her path and they gave way, leaving her teetering on a cliff that dropped sharply away to the sea and a rocky cove beneath.

Chapter Seven

Summer scanned the cove for the cat. It had disappeared.

There were plenty of places for it to have gone, Summer saw, as she took in the long curve of the land beneath her. Tumbled boulders lined the coast, as if a giant's child had upended his box of building bricks and left them, scattered. A small cat could easily disappear for good in between them.

I hope it's OK.

She shielded her eyes against the sun and looked out to the felt-tipped line of the horizon. Light danced off the water's surface in a million Christmas lights.

A picture-postcard scene. Perfect.

In her mind's eye she saw her mother, face tilted towards the sun, her hair blown back off her forehead, her eyes closed, smiling, drinking this in.

Did you ever stand here and look down at this, Mum?

Until she plucked up enough courage to talk to Tristan, she wouldn't know. Summer sighed. The questions she had had since her mother's death came crowding in again. Maybe Bosleven, the place, was not the key to her mother's decision to send her here. Maybe it was Tristan and his wife, Becca, who were important. But then why had her mother never mentioned them or the house? It was too weird to be sent to live with unknown relatives, people she had never even heard of – wasn't it?

Mum might have made her will before she'd even met Jess's mum. Maybe she never thought about changing it.

Perhaps her mother had broached the subject with Jess's parents once, Summer reasoned. Perhaps they had said no. She remembered how Jess had backed away from her, not being able to cope with her grief. It would not have worked, staying there.

It was no good. Too many maybes, too few clues. Thinking like this only brought more useless tears. She should not have run off like that. She needed to talk to Tristan.

I am an idiot. Idiot, idiot, idiot.

Summer took a deep shuddering breath and told herself to make a decision. She would climb down on to the rocks and find her way to the water's edge. It would be something to do to distract her.

She picked her way carefully down the side of the cliff and found her way to the far side of the beach. Rocks, rocks, rocks, as far as she could see to the left and right of her. A moonscape in bright sunlight. She tried tracing back in her mind the way she had come. Could she see the house from here? She looked up at the cliffs. No, she would have to be far out in a boat on the water to be able to see it. Which meant they wouldn't spot her either.

To the left, the bay curved round, framed by orange-red cliffs. A peak of bald rock jutted out, shielding the view of the rest of the coastline; the cliff there rising and falling in a craggy point. She imagined trying to climb it.

You'd need ropes and stuff. This is wild!

She glanced up at a helicopter going over, tried to envisage what she would look like to the pilot. She would be a speck in this landscape, if she was visible at all. She was tiny, insignificant.

I am alone now. Alone in the world.

The thought should have made her sad again, but as she inhaled the salty-sweet air, she felt free. She stretched and felt a pleasant pull along her spine. She was stronger, taller. Un-Summer-like.

Climbing across the rocks had been exhilarating. It was good to feel something physical, rather than the tears and tiredness of recent days. She checked to see no one was watching her, then raised her arms to the sky and threw her head back.

On top of the world!

She could hardly remember the last time she had seen the sea. There had been bucket-and-spade holidays as a little kid; she knew that, but remembered it only as though looking at a faded photograph. She tried to recapture the sensation of wading into the shallows, her hand held hotly in her mother's.

She closed her eyes, trying hard to focus, to hold on to that picture. She was already forgetting things about her mother. She was alarmed that she could not picture her face in detail.

And then I see her when she's not there.

Summer opened her eyes again and looked cautiously ahead.

Will I see you again?

She was beginning to feel heavy and melancholy once more, and berated herself for foolishly running away from the house.

What did you think you were doing?

She saw herself walk across the surface of the water before her, walk right to the edge, and then step off the planet. Falling, falling . . .

It would be good to fall. To disappear so that she did not have to deal with anything or feel anything any more.

She shook herself.

Need to do *something. Stop thinking.*

She edged forward, going as close to the water's edge as she dared, and plonked herself down on a high rock. It was warm. She lay back and spread herself on its pitted surface, soaking up the heat from the earth beneath her and the sun above. It was a different kind of heat from the sticky closeness of the city she had left behind: a cleaner, searing heat, as though she had been dropped on to a griddle pan.

She propped herself up on her elbows and looked down into the water.

So clear!

The rocks below formed a square pool. Summer leaned over and inspected the space more closely. It looked deliberately sculpted.

Could you cut into rock like that?

Peering down into the luminous water, she knew she had to dunk herself in it right away. It would probably be freezing, but she didn't care.

She kicked off her trainers and saw that blisters had formed in painful red welts on her heels and insteps.

Another swift check to make certain sure that she was alone, then she pulled her T-shirt over her head, tugged her jeans down. So what, if anyone saw her in her underwear? Then, before the sensible little voice inside her could insist that she get dressed and forget it, she sat on the edge of the pool and pushed herself off the side, slithering into the bright water.

She had known the water would be cold, but nothing could have prepared her for the iron grip that seized her lungs, squeezing the life out of her. She hauled herself out immediately and hopped from one foot to the other, holding her arms and whimpering. What had she expected?

Numpty! You haven't got a towel or anything.

She bunched up her jeans and gave herself a brisk rub down, scrambled back into her clothes, embarrassed at her stupidity. Then she sat, hunched and shivering as she looked out at the infinite sea.

How could the world carry on existing like this, so unfeeling? Her mum was dead, but nothing else had changed. The sun still rose, the clouds still gathered, the rain still fell, the tides kept coming in and out, in and out, day after day after day.

Summer had felt like this even more so in the days before the funeral: how *could* people drive cars, run to catch buses, eat takeaways, go to the cinema, as if her mother had never existed? It was so – *in your face*. It wasn't right. Surely her mum had made more of an impression on the earth? How could she have simply disappeared without a trace?

So did I see her back at the house, or what? And if I did . . . was it her watching me earlier?

She shook her head angrily.

I have got to stop this.

She stared and stared, fighting back the tears, wanting to blame someone, to shout and hit and scream and punch someone for the unfairness of it all.

The sea remained majestically beautiful; glittering and calm, unaffected by her emotions.

Had her mother sat here once, staring out to sea,

thinking, dreaming, laughing, talking with a friend? Holding hands? Maybe even in love?

Where did that *come from?*

Collecting her trainers, she crammed her sore feet back into them. Then, with one last heavy sigh, she started back to the house.

Chapter Eight

Summer hovered in the kitchen doorway. The clock above Tristan's head read five past four.

Her uncle was standing in the alcove, cooking something on a large, old-fashioned range. She coughed to get his attention.

He looked up sharply, a spoon half raised to his lips.

'Oh!' he breathed. 'You . . .'

She caught a fleeting look of alarm in his eyes as he dropped the spoon and fumbled to catch it.

He'd forgotten about me!

She was surprised by how much the thought upset her. After all, she felt nothing for this man other than resentment at the fact she was forced to live with him. But the idea that she might also mean so little to him – so little that he could simply forget she was in his house at all . . . it made her dizzy. She turned to leave.

Tristan immediately called her back. 'Summer!' he said. 'It's all right. I'm so sorry. You startled me. I was miles away! I was thinking about . . . Never mind. You've caught the sun already,' he said, covering his confusion with a smile, his head on one side.

Summer kept her face blank.

What do I say to him?

She had no idea how to bend the conversation round to the things she wanted to know. It was easier to stay silent.

Tristan carefully laid down the spoon. He looked up at her sheepishly, brushed his hands on the flowery apron he was wearing and laughed, 'I know, not a great look, is it?'

Summer's heart gave a little as she took in his bashful expression together with the ridiculous apron. She remained stubbornly silent, however, fighting the urge to laugh along with him.

Tristan fumbled for something to say. 'Ah, is – is Kenan with you? I was going to take you both into town but I couldn't find you. The day has rather run away with itself. Did you get any lunch? I suppose you did have a late breakfast—'

'Dunno where he is,' Summer cut in, terse and sullen.

'Oh? I thought you and he had gone off together. On a tour.' Tristan's brow furrowed. 'What happened?'

'Bit of a fight.'

'A fight—!'

'No, no I don't mean like a *fight*-fight,' Summer said.

Flip, he's going to wonder what kind of a nightmare he's got on his hands.

71

'Oh?'

'I mean . . . like a disagreement. It's nothing.'

Tristan looked genuinely upset. Summer felt a twinge of guilt.

'I'm so sorry, Summer,' he was saying, biting his lip. He pushed at his hair again. 'As I said, this has been a surprise for us – to have you come and live here like this. Kenan will be all right, he just needs a bit of time. As I'm sure you do too. Maybe I was wrong to throw you two together so quickly. He's used to his own space here.'

Summer nodded. ''S OK. I understand.'

I understand perfectly. I've upset poor little Kenan by just being here. I've clearly upset his mother, wherever she is. I've upset everyone.

'Plus, I'm not sure he's that comfortable around girls.' Tristan was doing that light-hearted, jokey thing again. 'My fault for sending him to an all-boys school! Which reminds me, we need to talk about school. There's a good one in Penzance. Might be the place to start. To take a look I mean . . .'

Summer shrugged.

There was another awkward silence, then they both started speaking at once.

'Well, maybe I should show you—'

'So when do I meet Becca?'

Tristan's face flushed suddenly. He looked as though she had slapped him. 'I . . . soon. She did pop through to get some stuff. You, er, you just missed her. Shame. She's a bit busy right now. You know how it is . . .' He turned back to stir a pot on the stove.

'Sure.' Summer scuffed at the wooden floor and stared at her feet. How was she going to get anything out of this man? Every opening she made was slammed shut again. Mum and she had talked, had shared everything.

Not quite everything. Not this place. Not Tristan and his family.

She was going to have to play along until he was ready. She tossed her hair, tried to look nonchalant. 'D'you want some help with that?'

Tristan looked over his shoulder.

She gestured to the pots simmering on the stove.

'No, no, that's fine. I'll stick it in here for a bit,' he said. He bent to transfer the pans into the oven. Then, straightening up, 'So where did Kenan take you? Before you . . . fell out.'

'Outside, mainly,' said Summer.

'Did he take you to the beach?'

'No.' Heat rose to her face. Should she say she had found it? Or thought she had?

'What about the rockery?' Tristan asked.

Summer looked at her feet, shrugged again. 'Dunno.'

What if he doesn't like me poking around on my own?

Tristan sighed. 'Oh dear. I had hoped he would be a bit more welcoming.'

'No, it's fine. I think he just had stuff to do . . .'

Great. He's going to have a go at Kenan. He'll really hate me then.

Tristan was taking off the apron and washing his hands. 'Right, well, I'll finish showing you round,' he said. 'Then I'll track Kenan down and have a word with him. You must go to the beach. Especially when the weather's like this. Going to be a hot one tomorrow too, so they say.'

'No, it's OK . . .'

But he wasn't listening. He had left the sink and turned to a door set into a recess to the left of the stove. She had not noticed it before.

As she followed Tristan, the little white cat scuttled past, nearly tripping her up.

'Oh! There you are.' Summer said softly, bending to stroke it, but it zipped away again before her fingers could brush its gleaming fur.

Tristan turned. 'What's that?' he asked.

'I was just saying hello to the cat . . .' she mumbled, embarrassed at being caught talking to the animal.

Tristan looked at her oddly. 'What?' He shook his head, frowned.

He doesn't want me here.

'Listen, you don't have to do this. If you're busy,' she said.

'No, no, of course not,' Tristan said. 'Let's go through

here first.' He turned the door knob.

Summer followed him into a small room with dark green, panelled walls. Overloaded bookcases, a higgledy-piggledy arrangement of comfy chairs and a couple of tables stacked with yet more books lent the room a cosy atmosphere. There was a woodburner set into the wall which backed on to the kitchen, and large French windows overlooking the garden. Summer saw they had a view across the lawn to the path where she had been earlier with Kenan.

'Can you see the sea?' Tristan said, coming over to stand beside her. 'There, through the pines,' he said, pointing between some tall, spindly trees.

Summer nodded as she glimpsed the water sparkling in the sunlight. She ran her tongue over her lips, tasting the salt.

'You can't always see it through those trees. If it's a grey day, or it's raining, the sea sort of merges into the sky and everything looks silvery,' he was saying. He paused, lost in thought. 'Anyway . . .' He blinked and turned. 'This is the little sitting room. Sometimes we call it the library, because of all the books. Obviously.' He chuckled. 'TV room too.' He pointed to the television, almost hidden behind a couple of chairs. 'We don't use it much when Kenan's not around. He watches stuff on his laptop anyway a lot of the time. I suppose you do that too?'

She pulled a face. 'Used to. On Mum's. Sometimes.'

Wonder if they'll send it on for me.

She had not wanted to go through her mum's stuff; had left that to Jess's parents. It had felt wrong, riffling through clothes and belongings – things that brought up such painful memories. She regretted it now. It would have been good to have had some of her mum's things with her.

Tristan looked at her uncomfortably: maybe she looked sad, thinking about her mother's possessions, or maybe it was the mere mention of her mother and the reminder of her death. 'Of – of course,' he stammered. 'Well, if you want to watch something here, go ahead. Obviously. Oh, and I should have said, do use the phone whenever you like. It's on the table in the hall. Mobiles don't work down here.'

'Thanks.'

Haven't got a mobile. Haven't got anyone to call.

He was moving away from the bookshelves now and looking towards the wall behind her. She turned and saw another door.

'Through there,' he said. 'The drawing room. It's, ah, it's a room we don't use that much, but I'll show you . . .' He excused himself as he slipped past her to open the door.

She gasped.

It was an enormous room! Almost as big as her old

house from top to bottom. The walls were covered in paintings. The chairs and table were arranged formally, neatly. Beyond them, at the far end of the room, was a giant beetle of a grand piano, the black and shining lid raised like wing casings as though it was about to take off. Summer moved towards it. It was the most beautiful instrument she had ever seen close to. It belonged in a concert hall, surely, not a family home?

She closed her eyes and was back in the huge auditorium, sitting next to her mother, transfixed by the man on the stage, his fingers flying over the brilliant black and white keys as his body swayed in time with his playing.

Her mother's face was a picture of bliss as she listened to the chords swelling and crashing in waves. What was the piece the pianist had played? She could remember the cascading arpeggios; if she reached out now she could touch her mother's hand . . .

'Summer? Summer!' Tristan was standing in front of her, alarmed, peering at her closely. 'Are you OK? Do you want to sit down?' He took her by the elbow. 'Oh dear, I should have taken time to make sure you were all right after that long journey. I should have . . . Oh dear.'

Summer sat down shakily in the chair Tristan had led her to. 'I – I'm fine. The piano . . . it reminded me . . .'

'Do you play?' Tristan asked, sitting down next to her. 'Ca— *Becca* did. Does, I mean! It's hers. I don't! Haven't got a musical bone in me, sadly. It's rather precious, though, the piano. It was Becca's father's. So I'm afraid that, er . . .' He was trying to find a polite way to warn her off.

'It's OK,' she reassured him. 'I wouldn't know one end from the other. I won't touch it. Mum played, but I never have.'

Her mother had promised to teach her that evening after the concert. 'One day,' she had said. 'When I have the money for a piano, that is.'

She had never had the time, let alone the money.

Summer glanced at the sleek instrument again.

'Your . . . mother played?' Tristan's voice was strained.

Why do people always behave as if they shouldn't mention her?

'She told me she used to. We didn't have a piano.'

He nodded. 'Shame when people give up, isn't it?'

They sat looking at one another in silence for a moment. Then Tristan was on his feet again and making an effort to resume his chatty tone from earlier. 'So I'll show you the rest of the place, shall I? If you're up to it.'

He went out of the room by another door which opened into the passage where Kenan had taken her that morning.

'This is the kitchen passage I was talking about last night,' he said.

'I know.'

'Oh, right. So you got this far with Kenan, then?'

'We went down here to get outside. I love the walled bit where the vegetables are. It's like *The Secret Garden*,' she said, suddenly shy.

'That's what your— Becca says that,' Tristan said, smiling.

'Kenan says she's a good gardener. I mean, it's obvious she is. Are you – do you do the garden too? I've always thought it must be cool to be able to grow things.' Now she had started talking, it was easier to keep going. She went on in a rush, 'Mum was brilliant at growing stuff. All my own things died, but she could grow anything, even on our little balcony. Sunflowers, tomatoes, the kind of thing you could fit into pots. She would love this place. I . . . I was wondering if she had ever been here? It's just no one's told me why—'

There was a sudden thumping noise from beyond the wall.

Summer looked up sharply. 'What was that?'

Tristan's face had gone white. 'Kenan probably,' he said.

Summer was not convinced. The sound had come from the exact same place she had heard noises that morning with Kenan. She opened her mouth to say so, but Tristan was already speaking again.

'Look, if you've been here with Kenan already, I'm sure you don't want to see all this again. It's only storerooms now, I'm sure he told you that.' Tristan was moving her quickly along. 'We don't need all this space with only three of us here. Used to be used for holiday lets, years ago. Have you seen the rest of upstairs?' He changed the subject abruptly, turned on his heel without waiting for her to reply and went back to the hall.

What's up with him? Was he spooked by those noises too?

Summer hurried to catch up. 'Kenan told me there were ghosts at Bosleven,' she said, determined to keep him talking.

Tristan gave a snort of laughter. 'Did he now?'

Summer frowned. 'Yeah. Do you think that's what that noise was, back there?'

'Of course not.' Tristan tutted. 'As I said, probably Kenan. He does crash about rather. Sounds like a herd of elephants when he runs around upstairs! Where did you say he went after you two argued?'

'I already told you, I don't know!' Summer felt irritated by his sudden brisk manner.

'It's easy to hide away in this place. He's probably in his room.' Her uncle stopped at the bottom of the stairs. His expression softened. 'Listen, I'm sorry about Kenan. I'll have a word with him, I promise. I'm sure he hasn't meant to upset you. He shouldn't have teased you about ghosts, and he certainly shouldn't have run away from you. This is a big, old, creaky house, that's all. Most of the noises you're hearing are wooden beams and floorboards. They contract and expand with changes in the weather. Old houses are like that.'

'S'pose.'

Tristan smiled. 'Since you ask, I'm not sure what I think about ghosts,' he said. 'I suppose I would have to say, if pushed, that I do believe in them. I just don't think they're white, headless spectres that jump out at you and go, "Whoooo!"' He laughed.

'So what do you believe?'

Tristan thought for a moment, then, 'I believe in – energy, for want of a better word,' he said. 'That people leave something of themselves behind when they go. I've always thought this place is full of that kind of thing. Bosleven, I mean. It's the sort of place that's hard to leave. The house, the gardens, everything.' He sounded dreamy. 'At least, *I* would find it hard to leave, I know that. Whenever I'm away, I can only think of being back. It's like I'm drawn here, on the end of an invisible thread. Becca thinks her mum and dad are still part of Bosleven.' He swallowed. His dark eyes were brimming with sadness. 'I think it's rather comforting to think of people belonging somewhere, even after they've gone.' He glanced at Summer again, 'I – I'm sorry, I don't want to upset you. Stupid of me to talk like this so soon after—'

'It's OK,' Summer said. 'I think I know what you mean.'

Before he had said all that, she had been ready to push him, to say, 'You can talk about Mum, you know. I'm not going to flip out on you!' But now that he was talking to her properly for the first time, she was simply relieved not to be laughed at or ignored. It was much better him talking like this than trying to avoid mentioning her mother's death altogether.

Her stomach filled up with butterflies. This was the perfect opportunity to tell Tristan about the phone call and the sight of her mother in the porch. If he did believe in this 'energy' he talked about, maybe he would have an explanation. The words built up and up inside her before she had the guts to force them out.

'I . . . I wanted to ask you something,' she began.

'Yes?'

'Do you think that the dead can contact the living? Like, directly, I mean. With special messages?' Summer immediately felt self-conscious, but Tristan was watching her intently, so she pressed on. 'It's – it's Mum, you see. I've been trying to figure everything out, cos no one's told me why I'm here. She – Mum – must have had a reason for sending me here. I mean, I know we're related and you're my guardian and everything, but I think it's more than that. I think it's Bosleven that was important to her somehow. It must be that, mustn't it? If we're only related distantly, or whatever? She never mentioned this place to me, though. So – do *you* know? Did she live here once? Or spend holidays here, or—'

'I don't know,' Tristan said. His expression had stiffened.

I've jumped in too soon. I should've waited. Maybe he wants to talk to me with Kenan and Becca.

'Right,' she said, reddening. 'I just thought you might be able to tell me a bit more. I mean, no one explained anything. Just said it was in the will . . .'

'I know this is a very hard time for you.' Tristan chose his words carefully. 'I can only say that I am sure your mother knew what she was doing. It was better for you to come here and be with relatives, even relatives you hadn't met, than to be sent into care – which is what would have happened otherwise, I suppose.' He stopped, realizing, perhaps, that he had gone too far.

'I – I hadn't thought of that.' Summer felt winded.

'I'm sorry,' he said. 'But you asked, and that is the only reason I can give for your mother naming us as your guardians.' He touched her lightly on her shoulder. 'So. Shall we go on?'

'What?' Summer frowned.

'Round the rest of the house,' said Tristan. He gestured up the stairs.

'Oh. Yeah.' She was piecing together some of his earlier comments. 'So . . . this house was *Becca's* family's? Not yours? Only you said Becca thought her mum and dad were still part of the place? And that her dad had given her the piano.'

'No. That's right. It's Becca's. I mean, she lived here as a child. She always said she wanted to come back here. Raise her own family. When her mother died, it just seemed the right thing to do.' He paused. 'Like I said, it has that effect on people. Bosleven, I mean. Draws people in.'

'So Becca didn't have any brothers or sisters, then?' Summer asked.

Tristan gave a small gasp, hurriedly checked his watch and said, 'I've left those pots stewing for far too long. Sorry, Summer. Must go and rescue the cooking or you'll be having toast for supper! Why don't you poke around upstairs on your own?' He was backing out of the door. 'Sorry!' he called again as he rushed into the kitchen, leaving Summer alone again for the second time that day.

Chapter Nine

Summer idled her way up the stairs, stopping on each step. A ray of light streamed in through a high window, dust motes shimmering and swirling before her.

What if that sunbeam were an opening into the past? Maybe I'd get some answers if I could go back.

She wished she could let herself be hypnotized by the swirling glitter in the golden shaft of light, forget reality and lose herself in fancy and make-believe as she used to when she was small. But she was unsettled, on edge, and her conversation with Tristan had done nothing to help.

He talked about 'energy'. About people leaving something of themselves behind.

Perhaps all that she had seen – her mother in the porch, the voice on the phone – had been simple projections; fulfilment of a deep-seated wish to have her mother back. Or at least to know that her mother had truly intended her to belong here.

She thought about what Tristan himself had said about belonging. About Bosleven drawing him back whenever he was away.

So, Mum. Have you been drawn back somehow?

How could she find out when her mother had been there? And where did Tristan's wife fit into all this if Bosleven was *her* family home? Had her mother and Becca been good friends? If so, why was Tristan named as her guardian, and not Becca? Where *was* Becca anyway?

Summer did not buy Tristan's explanation about his wife being too busy to meet her. Surely the arrival of an unknown girl into the family would be enough to bring any normal person away from their work or whatever it was her aunt was so busy with, if only out of curiosity? She could not imagine her own mother staying away at such a time.

Maybe if I look around carefully, I'll pick up some clues.

She clearly would not find out anything if she remained hanging about, dreaming like this.

She reached the half-landing where Tristan had said his room was. There were three doors ahead of her. Even though Tristan had said she could look around on her own, she felt like an intruder.

He has tried to be kind, though. Unlike Kenan.

Thinking of her cousin again made her hesitate. She didn't want to come across him up here so soon after he had told her to 'piss off'. She listened to the house.

Silence, apart from the odd sigh and whisper of floorboards and creaking beams.

She thought of Tristan saying Kenan thumped around 'like a herd of elephants'. No way was he back. The place was too quiet. Even a geek like him would listen to music in his room. She stayed on the landing, listening.

She was distracted by a glance up at the main landing. The door to her own room, at the end, was open a crack. Hadn't she closed it earlier?

Thoughts of Kenan's ghostly stories returned. She pushed them away and resolutely skipped up the last few stairs. Nevertheless she darted into her room quickly, as though to surprise an intruder. If Kenan was lurking, ready to jump out, she would not give him the pleasure of spooking her.

There was no one. She noted guiltily that she had left it in rather a mess; the bed covers thrown back in a muddled heap, her nightclothes tangled on the floor. The contents of her rucksack were spilling out too. She stared at the books, photos in frames and spare clothes poking out of the top of the bag.

S'pose I should unpack.

She went over to the rucksack and bent down to pick up her things. Then doubt crept into her mind.

Did I really leave everything like this?

She pushed back the niggling thought: that someone – something? – had rummaged through her belongings. No. She shook her head: she was simply tired, letting paranoia get the better of her. Ghosts belonged to myths and fairy tales, and in any case they did not look through people's possessions.

Summer picked up the photos: one of her with her mum and one with Jess. The first one had a crack across the glass.

She ran her finger over the hairline break. Both photo frames had been wrapped in T-shirts to protect them while she had travelled.

He has been in here.

Hot, prickling anger rose from the pit of her stomach. She could just see Kenan doing that, coming into her room after he had left her in the garden, rootling through her stuff, finding the photo and throwing it down without a care for her feelings or privacy.

You rat – wait till I get my hands on you!

How could she prove it, though? Tristan was hardly likely to believe his son would do such a thing. She had no evidence, no witness. It would be her word against his.

She seethed as she set both frames gently on the bedside table. She told herself to calm down, that at least it was only a crack, nothing more. She gazed at the photo. It was her favourite one of her mum: Catherine had her head thrown back in that way she had when she laughed, hair blowing across her face, one arm around Summer. Jess had taken it at the Christmas fairground in Hyde Park. And the other photo was of Jess, sitting on her bed, cross-legged, grinning like a loony.

A little bit of home. She stroked the frames as a knot of sadness caught in her chest.

Jess. Thought we'd be friends forever.

It was over. Jess had been unable to hide her relief as she waved Summer off at Paddington. Jess belonged to another time, another life.

She turned the photo face down.

She went back to look for her iPod, eager to fill her mind with music, to empty it of thought. She emptied out the contents of her rucksack: T-shirts, swimming costume (not that she'd be swimming in *that* water again!), another pair of jeans, underwear, some books, a notepad, pens. No iPod came to light.

Where is it?

Summer distinctly remembered putting it away before getting off the train. It had been such a precious gift from her mother, who had saved and saved for it, she knew that.

He's taken that as well.

She knew then that she had to do something, to get Kenan back, to prove what a snoop he was.

She hurried out of her room and down the landing. She made straight for Kenan's room, remembering Tristan had pointed it out the night before. A laptop was open on the desk, its screen dark but its blue lights winking, ready for action at the touch of a finger. So tempting.

Facebook! Bet he's said something to his mates about me.

She might find something that would show Tristan what his son had been up to, really get him into trouble . . .

Excitement prickled as she looked over her shoulder, listening closely for footsteps. When she heard none she let her fingers fall lightly on to the mouse-pad. The screen flashed to life, drawing a sharp breath from Summer as she realized what she had revealed.

. . . won't be for long. Just until I get my head straight. Be patient. I know it's hard. Hugs, Mum xxxx

The end of a message from his mum! Underneath it, the beginnings of a reply from Kenan. Summer looked at the date and time Becca's message had been sent. Earlier in the morning. Kenan must have been in the middle of replying when he had been called to have breakfast and then forced to show her around. Was that why he had been so resentful? He had wanted to go and see his mum, not act as tour guide. Maybe he'd run straight to see his mum after shouting at Summer.

She eagerly began to read. Her anger at Kenan's behaviour silenced the nagging voice that told her she was the snoop now.

Mum, why did you fight about her coming? I want to know the *real* reason. I know you said about the will, but so what? Doesn't tell us who she really is, does it? And why should that make you so mad at Dad? He's gone all weird and quiet. He's either cooking all the time or in his study and he won't tell me what's going on. I wish she'd never come to

Soft padding footsteps on the landing caused Summer to start away from the screen, mid-sentence.

She raced to the door, but reached it only in time to hear another door slam. She peeked out. There was no one there.

There were some books on the floor, though, by the bookcase outside her room. Had they been there before? Had they been knocked from the shelves by someone rushing past?

Summer's nerves were jangling now. She made herself look carefully up and down the landing. Had someone been watching her? If so, it could not have been Kenan: he would surely have rushed at her the minute he saw her in his room, reading his personal correspondence. He would have shouted abuse, not spied on her and scuttled away.

The house was quiet. There was no one anywhere nearby.

Summer felt shame wash through her. She was the

one at fault, not Kenan. She had intruded on her cousin's privacy; judged him too harshly. He was not a mean, bullying character, he was simply a boy who missed his mother, who was upset that his parents had been fighting – because of her. He understood just as little as she did the reasons why he had to share his life with some unknown relative.

Maybe they had more in common than either of them would be willing to admit.

She hovered in the doorway and glanced back at the laptop. Sunlight caught on an object on the bed, grabbing her attention.

An iPod. Same silver facing as hers. Same white protective backing.

So he did nick it!

She went over and picked it up, touching the button at the base of the screen. A song she didn't recognize.

Not mine. Just a coincidence then.

She flicked through the music.

A couple of albums of stuff she would never have listened to in a million years; hard-core guitars and loads of mad, shouty screaming.

Had he really got the exact same iPod as hers? Or had he pinched hers and wiped it, replacing it with some of his own rubbish taste in music? She put it in the pocket of her hoody, then immediately withdrew it and threw it back on to the unmade bed, clenching her teeth in frustration.

92

If I take it, he'll know I've been in here. If I don't take it, he might have got away with it.

No iPod, no phone, no computer. Cut off from the whole of the outside world.

Who would I contact anyway?

Her stomach growled. She remembered she had not eaten anything since her late breakfast of a small bowl of cereal.

I'll have to go downstairs if I'm not going to starve.

She sighed.

And I'll have to ask about where Becca is. I need to know.

Chapter Ten

Kenan was there for supper, which they ate early. He sat in silence through most of the meal, ignoring Summer completely and only rewarding his father's gentle probing questions with a grunt or two.

Summer was still churning about the cracked photo frame and the iPod, in spite of feeling sorry for Kenan after reading the messages. His attitude towards her did not help: he was still so hostile. It would not be ridiculously far-fetched to imagine him snooping in her room, stealing from her. But why?

Just to be mean probably.

She had made a promise to herself: she wouldn't say anything to him until she had more proof, and certainly not in front of Tristan. She forced polite conversation about how lovely the food was: vegetables from the garden, apparently, and fish pie, made from catch of the day, bought in the nearby village of Newlyn.

Eventually the conversation dried up. Summer concentrated on the scrape of knives and forks on plates.

A phone rang.

Tristan jumped.

Is no one going to answer it?

It was not coming from the hall where Tristan had said the phone was. It sounded as though it was coming from the other end of the kitchen passage.

'Office phone,' Tristan said sharply. 'It can wait.'

The ringing stopped.

Tristan and Kenan exchanged a glance.

'So if you're done with the fish pie, I thought strawberries and cream? Clotted cream, of course. From the farm,' Tristan said, bright and chatty, as he gathered their cutlery and dishes.

Kenan remained silent.

The harsh, rasping call of rooks filled the air. Summer looked out at them as they flew across the lawn to roost in messy nests in the top of the pines.

'Do they always make that noise?' she asked, more for something to say than because she wanted to know.

'It's a racket, isn't it?' said Tristan.

'Oh, no. I like it,' Summer said. She knew she sounded overeager. 'It's kind of comforting. Like they're saying the day's over but they'll always be there, or something.'

'Oh, right, so you don't believe in ghosts, but all of a sudden you can speak bird language?' Kenan said, jeering.

Summer felt the blood rush to her face. 'No, I—'

'Kenan,' Tristan said.

'Well, I hate them,' Kenan said with feeling. 'They wake me up too early. There's far too many of them now. Can't we shoot some of them, Dad?'

Summer's spine tingled as she took in the spiteful look on her cousin's face.

He can't always be like this. Look at how he wrote to his mum. It's me. My fault.

'I don't think it's a great idea to kill an animal just because you find them annoying,' Tristan said quietly. 'Anyway, you've never told me before that they wake you.'

'Not as though you'd listen if I did,' Kenan muttered. He rocked back on his chair, studiously avoiding eye contact with his father.

'Kenan, what's got into you?' Tristan threw the words out in exasperation. 'Can't you at least be pleasant while we're sharing a meal together? You've said nothing all evening and Summer says you left her—'

Summer cut in quickly, raising her voice to prevent the argument escalating. 'The phone. It reminded me . . . I – I wanted to ask you,' she said. 'I haven't got a mobile—'

Kenan snorted, breaking out of his sulk to rock forward with a jibe. 'Wouldn't be much point anyway. There's no signal here, is there? Flipping black hole, this place.'

'Kenan!' Tristan remonstrated. 'Please.' His chair was

harsh on the bare boards as he pushed it away and went to get the dessert.

'What d'you mean?' Summer said to her cousin. 'You're not telling me *you* don't have a mobile?'

Kenan curled his lip.

Tristan answered. 'We do, but I'm afraid Kenan's right. I did say, I think, didn't I? We can't get a signal here in the house or in the garden. You can get one in St Gerran – sometimes you get a faint one on the farm road. But it's hopeless here.'

'Oh.'

'When we go into town we can send texts and so on,' Tristan assured her. 'I'll get you one next time we go into Penzance, don't worry. I know how important it is. But in the meantime, like I said, please do use the phone in the hall. Any time.'

Like I'm going to do that with both of you listening.

'Thanks.'

'And if you have a laptop—'

'I don't,' Summer said. 'I told you.'

Kenan shot her a nasty smile. 'Shame.'

'Maybe Summer could borrow yours—?'

'No way,' Kenan snapped.

'You mean like he's "borrowed" my iPod?' Summer spoke over her cousin.

'WHAT?' Kenan slammed his hands on the table and reared up out of his chair.

Summer was shaking; anger pulsed through her. 'I said,' she said deliberately, '"You mean like he's 'borrowed' my iPod?"'

Kenan leaned over the table and grabbed her by the shoulders.

'HEY!' Tristan rushed over and pulled Kenan back. 'What's going on?'

Kenan shook his father off and shouted, 'Why don't you ask her? She's the one accusing me of theft!'

Summer raised her eyebrows. She was fizzing with anger, but determined to stay calm and in control. 'That's not actually what I said. But you did go into my room, didn't you? My photo frame's smashed too,' she added, knowing she was exaggerating, not caring.

'That's enough. Sit down, Kenan,' Tristan instructed. 'We can't discuss anything with you both about to jump at each other's throats.'

'Forget it,' Kenan spat. 'I'm not discussing anything with anyone. 'Specially not *her*.' He wheeled away from his father, catching the edge of the work surface and sending the plates and cutlery clattering to the floor. 'I'm going out.'

Tristan opened his mouth to speak, but Kenan had gone. Summer's uncle looked washed out. The skin around his eyes was dark, leaving them sunken and old. The lines on his face seemed etched more deeply.

'What on earth was that all about?' Tristan shook his head.

Summer said nothing.

Tristan put his hands on his hips. 'I think you have to try to understand, Summer, that this is tricky for Kenan too. Please try.'

'Yeah, well. At least his mum's not dead,' Summer said. She kept her gaze steady. 'So, yes, I'm sure it's all very difficult for you to have someone turn up into your cosy lives in your mansion and upset everything but I can tell *you* that being told you have to go and live with people you know nothing about, who've never even been mentioned to you in passing, to have to leave everything and everyone you know . . .' She paused, her lungs tight. 'Well, it's . . . it's . . .' She was not going to cry in front of him.

As her vision blurred, she turned on her heel and ran, not stopping until she was in her room, the door slammed behind her.

Chapter Eleven

Summer woke early the next morning. She had fallen asleep the night before overcome by great shuddering sobs; unable to stem the flow, she had muffled the crying with her pillow. There was no way she would let Kenan hear her.

Now, as she shifted in the high bed and came to slowly, the memory of the previous day leaked back into her, bringing with it a bruised heaviness to her eyes.

She wanted to pull sleep back over her, but she was awake now and had to face what the day had in store. So she got up and drew the curtains. The sea winked a greeting over the tops of the pine trees, its surface dove-grey, tempting, speckled with sharp points of silver.

What if I called Jess? Tristan did say I could use the phone.

A few minutes of connection with her old home: a raft, a lifeline. But she knew that if she heard her friend's voice, she would only break down and become a wreck again. Jess would react exactly how she had in the days after Catherine's death: embarrassed and helpless. In any case it was too early to phone now. Jess had never been an early riser.

At least I can be up and out before I have to face them.

She had already decided to go back down to the rocks. She packed her small bag with her swimming costume (for sunbathing purposes only, she thought, remembering the icy cold water) and a towel from the bathroom.

Once out on the landing, she remembered with a quiver what she had heard and seen the day before: the soft footsteps, the books lying on the floor. She checked the bookcase, listening intently for a hint of anyone hovering nearby, but the books were all in place and there was no noise apart from the usual creaks and sighs from the old house.

Summer told herself not to be ridiculous. She ran quickly down the stairs, however, into the reassuring warmth and light of the kitchen.

She should take some food down to the rocks. She plucked an apple from a bowl on the dresser and found a bread roll in a bin on the worktop. In the fridge were a few litre cartons of juice with screw-top lids, so she took one that was half full and stuffed it in her bag along with the food.

Summer was running through the silent garden – the 'rockery' Tristan had referred to. She felt lighter the further away from the house she went. The stones beneath her feet were slippery glass, drenched with sunlight and freezing-clean spring water. She skipped over them, stepping in the stream, letting her feet get wet. It didn't matter. She wasn't going to stop there.

She ran on to open space, the sea, thoughts rippling through her mind.

Could I run away? Have I got the guts?

She kept running until she reached the cliff path. She was more nimble over the rocks this time, knowing that she was unlikely to slip on the dry boulders that were above the tideline.

Summer found herself smiling as she looked out over the glistening water. At least she had found this place. This would be her refuge. The house was no good – not while Kenan was there. Not while something was watching her.

She made herself focus on the fantasy film-set before her, pushing aside her fears and anxiety. This was a place where anything could happen, she told herself. It was so far away from her own, hemmed-in, grey, sad existence.

What if she could stay here?

I could camp! They wouldn't miss me. Be relieved I'd gone. I could bring stuff down – tins, matches, blankets.

Even as she thought these words, full of bravado, she knew she'd never do it. Camping with her mum to organize everything, to remember all the equipment and know how to pitch a tent and light a campfire, that was one thing; managing alone was quite another.

Summer laughed out loud at herself, feeling giddy with the joy of being on the beach, alone, early in the day. This was hers, all hers! So what if she couldn't survive like a hermit, holed up in a cave, catching her own fish, gutting it, cooking it . . . She could enjoy just being there.

She whirled round, the bay spinning before her. A merry-go-round of happiness.

Sitting down to catch her breath, she watched as the sea constantly played tricks on the eye, its shifting, lapping surface throwing up dark shapes and strange angles. It made her remember a holiday on Dartmoor a few years back. Her mother had promised her 10p for every different type of bird she spotted and named. She hadn't got past 'blue tit', 'blackbird' and 'buzzard'.

She squinted at the waves, scanning the bay, willing something to appear, anything. A sign of life other than her own.

She had been staring right at a dark shape ahead of her for a full minute without registering what it was, vaguely thinking it was another rock peeking over the silky, still surface. Then it turned. It looked at her, full in the face.

'Oh!' Her hands flew to her mouth.

The dark, dog-like head stared back steadily, coolly.

A seal!

Summer stopped short of clapping her hands in childish delight, her mouth stretched wide with joy, her eyes watering.

A real, live, seal!

She got up and went to the edge of the rocky ledge, not thinking about slipping and falling now. The seal didn't budge, didn't seem at all bothered by her presence; merely gazed serenely back as if to say, 'Nice day for it.'

Summer sat herself down again and swung her legs over the steep side of the highest rock. She had an urge to struggle into her costume and plunge in, to swim up to the seal, to touch it, her earlier qualms about entering the freezing water swept away by her excitement.

She was so caught up in the moment, everything else around her had faded away; it was just her and the seal, staring at each other, like two kids on the school bus, too shy to talk.

'Hey!'

For the tiniest moment, Summer thought the seal had spoken.

'Hey! Hello!'

Summer turned and saw a figure making its way quickly across the rocks from the cliff path towards her. Her heart began thudding in her chest. She should have known this place belonged to someone. That's why it was so difficult to get down here from the cliffs; someone wanted to keep it private. Now she was going to get caught. There was nowhere to go, however, even if she could race over the craggy surface of the beach. She eyed the caves. The figure was already leaping and bounding from rock to rock, as sure-footed as a cat hopping from roof to roof. How did this person manage to move so fast?

Summer turned back to the seal. It had disappeared beneath the waves. She sat, frozen. There was nowhere for her to hide.

'Oh!' said the stranger, close behind her now. 'The seal! I wondered what you were looking at.'

The voice didn't sound threatening. Summer peered at its owner over one shoulder.

The face, now level with hers, was beaming; both friendly and curious. Summer felt a rush of heat as she took in the brown, smooth cheeks; glass-blue eyes, as clear as the rock pools; a small nose sprinkled with a scattering of dark brown freckles. The smile was broad, innocent, showing glimpses of straight, bright, white teeth. The face was topped off with a messy mop of sun-bleached blond hair.

She wanted to hide what she knew was a blush forming.

'Hi,' said the boy.

'Hi,' Summer croaked back. She looked into eyes the colour of the sea, framed by absurdly long, brown eyelashes. The urge to hide her face was almost overpowering, but she forced herself to hold his gaze.

'Been for a swim yet?' The voice was deeper than Kenan's, but nevertheless betrayed its recent change from a higher pitch, and there was a softness to it; the words rolled in his mouth, the 'r's especially rounded. 'Not seen you down here before. On holiday?' he continued.

'Something like that,' she said.

The boy sat down beside her, dangling his long brown legs next to hers. 'I'm Zach. You?'

Summer sniffed and said, 'Summer,' keeping her voice as casual as she could.

'So, Summer – how d'you find the beach? Not many people make it down. Difficult to find. But then, I guess – that's kind of obvious . . .' Zach tailed off and looked away again, swinging his legs gently, bouncing his heels off the rocks.

Thought so. He's going to tell me I am trespassing.

'I, like . . . found it by accident,' Summer said.

Zach smiled. 'So you came on your own?'

Summer shrugged, a smile flickering on her own lips now. She should play it cool. Especially if he was about to tell her she had to go.

'Oh, I get it. Wanted to get away.' Zach nodded. 'Like that all the time in the holidays. I can never wait to get away, myself. Can't find me any jobs to do if I'm here, eh? So you've met the seal?' he pressed on, in spite of Summer's reticence. 'Amazing, that guy. Fearless. You

106

can swim with him, you know. He won't hurt. He'd never let you get close enough. He's just curious. All seals are curious. Well, a lot of them are.'

Summer felt fidgety in the face of all this banter. She was unused to anyone showing any interest in her. Especially a boy.

'You do swim, don't you?' Zach asked, breaking into her thoughts.

Summer remained silent.

'Where are you from?' Zach persisted.

This was too much for Summer.

Where am I from? Not from round here, that's for sure.

She got up clumsily. 'What's with all the questions?' she snapped. 'Can't I just sit here without someone coming and asking me what I'm doing, who I am, where I've come from? I came here to get away from everything.'

Zach had pulled back, confused. 'Sorry – I didn't mean—' he stammered.

Summer was annoyed with herself. Annoyed with this boy for turning up and asking all those questions, just when she had found somewhere she could be alone. When was she going to stop being such a nightmare, to act normal again? This boy had done nothing wrong, but she found she could not stop herself from lashing out at him.

'I just want to be left alone!' she cried, turning from him.

'OK. I'm sorry,' he repeated. He was concerned, not angry, as Summer felt he should have been.

'I'm going,' she spat, and scooped up her bag and towel. She did not want any more questions.

No one's got answers to any of my *questions, have they?*

She was lurching over the rocks, her blood churning in her ears.

'Careful!' Zach called after her. 'You'll fall!'

She slowed a little, but kept her eyes fixed on the path up to the clifftop. Soon she was in the woods. She stopped and scanned the way she had come. He hadn't followed. She was alone.

When she got back to the house, the clouds had evaporated and Bosleven was already bright, lit up by the sun, now high overhead. The air up here was still, the heat more intense away from the coast.

Summer stayed in the shade of the path at the bottom of the garden, trailing her feet in the dust and kicking idly at dried leaf mould. Her head ached. She licked her lips and tried not to think of ice cubes knocking together in a long tall glass of cool water. She imagined what it would feel like to enter the damp, chilly kitchen, to lean against the cold, white-ceramic side of the sink and let the tap water run over her wrists.

She could not go in right away. Someone would see her, notice how hot and bothered she was, see she was flustered, ask more questions. She needed time to calm down.

'There you are!'

Too late. She emerged, hangdog, from the shadows to see Tristan was walking across the lawn, waving cheerily.

'You were up early,' he said. Then, taking in her bag and messily bunched-up towel, 'Kenan told you how to get to the beach then. Been for a swim?'

'Er, no.'

So he's not going to mention last night's outburst?

It seemed that Tristan was waiting for her to say more. When she didn't he said, 'So. You did well to find the beach on your own.'

'Yeah?'

'The beach is the best thing about this place,' he said. 'Did I tell you it's, ah, it's our beach?' He looked bashful.

'*Your* beach?'

'Yes, well. In theory. We can't exactly police it, but we keep it tricky to find!' He laughed. 'Anyway, when I'm not busy I like to go down for a dip. You have to be careful where you get in and out. The rocks, you know. It's helpful to know the tides. We've got a little book that tells you when high and low tides are – I'll show you.'

So it is *private. Does that boy know? Is that why he*

was so nosy? Maybe he thought I'd tell . . .

Summer knew she must be blushing as she held an image of Zach in her mind for a second.

Tristan was still talking. 'Kenan'll go down with you later. You'll be safe with him. Wouldn't like to think of you swimming alone – not just yet. You need to get used to the swell around the rocks, that kind of thing.'

Summer raised her eyebrows. She did not think she and Kenan would be having friendly little seaside picnics together any time soon.

'Give him a chance?' Tristan said, as though reading her thoughts.

'Mmm,' she mumbled.

'Breakfast.' Tristan nodded towards the house. 'Oh, by the way – I found this.' He was holding something out to her, something which caught the sunlight and reflected it back in a sudden white blaze.

Summer let out a tiny gasp. 'My iPod!'

'It was in the car, on the back seat. It was so dark when we got here . . .'

'Thanks.' Kenan was definitely going to hate her now. She had rushed to accuse him and he would know she had been in his room.

She pressed the button at the base of the screen. Nothing. Out of power.

Tristan picked up the thread of what he'd been saying about Kenan. 'He's not what you'd call a morning person, generally,' he said. 'I suppose that's why I was surprised to see you up and about. I thought all teenagers liked a lie-in! But then, what do I know, eh?' His kind eyes twinkled. 'Come on, you look as though you could use a drink. Amazing how hot it is already today, isn't it?'

She smiled, grateful that he clearly was not going to comment on the scene she had provoked with his son the night before.

He is all right.

Once they were in the kitchen, Tristan went over to fridge and brought an ice cube tray out of the freezer compartment.

'Water OK?' he asked. 'Or d'you prefer juice?' He turned back to the fridge.

'I don't mind,' Summer said. She sat down at the table and stared out at the sea.

Tristan came back with the water, and some juice in a carton.

'I'll fix some food in a minute.' He handed her the glass, rattling with ice. He looked suddenly earnest. 'I want you to know that I understand what it's like to lose someone as you've done,' he said. 'I know how utterly dreadful it is. How confusing and . . . the only thing I don't know,' he went on carefully, 'is what to say to you at the moment. In fact, I think in many ways it's best if I don't say too much. I can't make things better. I think you need time and space, and that's what I plan on giving you. Unless you want to talk, of course?' He bit his lip. 'I know we chatted a bit about – about, well . . . in a more general way, didn't we? But if you want to talk more about your mum . . .' He tailed off.

Summer shook her head. While he had been speaking, she had felt that familiar welling-up begin again, deep inside her. It roared through her, filling her head with wordless, painful noise, pushing to the surface until she couldn't fight it, couldn't push it back any more.

She heard Tristan grab a chair and sit next to her. She felt him take her into his arms. Her grief was like something separate from her, stronger than her. It came with no warning, knocking the ground from under her. She was no longer Summer, the girl who had had friends and laughed and told jokes and lived a normal life: that girl was spirited away, spiralling into darkness while a raging sadness took hold of her.

His being so kind – that only made everything worse. He would never be what her mother had been to her.

Mum, Mum, Mum.

Somewhere in the background, behind the terrible, animal noise she was making, she was aware of her uncle's voice, crooning, telling her it was all right, he understood, she should let it all out, have a good cry. That she would feel better when she did.

But I won't, will I? I will never feel better.

'That looks cosy. Can I join in?'

Summer pulled away from Tristan, his shirt soaked with her salty tears. She swiped at her mouth, eyes and nose, furiously rearranged her features.

Her cousin was standing in the doorway. He stared at her, his eyes like flint.

'Don't mind me,' Kenan drawled, deliberately pushing past Summer and his father. 'I'll sort myself out.' He grabbed a plate and went to get some bread out of the bin on the worktop. He yanked a drawer open, pulled out a knife and began hacking at the loaf.

Tristan opened his mouth as if about to rebuke his son for his insensitivity, but seemed to think better of it.

Why does he always let him get away with being such a mouthy little—?

'Listen, Summer, why don't you go to my office? Use my laptop if you like? I'll come up with a cup of tea.'

'Thanks.' She heard her voice, cracked, distant.

'OK,' said Tristan. 'You know where it is? Next to my room. You have some peace and quiet for a bit.'

He gave her another quick hug.

Summer nodded gratefully and turned away, leaving Kenan hissing in fury, already tearing strips off Tristan.

'What were you thinking of, *hugging* her like that? After everything Mum said . . . !'

Spoilt. Horrible. Evil . . .

When she got upstairs, the door to the office was ajar.

She pushed at it gently, still shaking, struggling to get a hold on herself.

Must concentrate, make the most of this.

Kenan was going to be on her case now more than ever, she knew it. This might be the only bit of 'peace and quiet' she would get for a long time.

Chapter Twelve

The office was a tip. Papers cascading from drawers, files bursting with paperwork, on an armchair, on the desk. In the middle of the chaos, the computer.

Summer thought of her mum's small table where she had worked, dealt with correspondence. It had always been cleared at the end of the day. If Summer had wanted to do her homework there, she had had to promise she would leave everything as she had found it.

She eyed the paperwork surrounding her and realized with a flicker of shame that she had not thought to ask her uncle anything about his life; what his job was. He seemed to be around a lot, although he had said he was busy and had mentioned having work to do.

Maybe he has his own business, works from home.

She went to the desk and flipped up the lid of the laptop. The homepage glowed invitingly. It crossed her mind that she could take a look at his browsing history.

Might give me some clues.

But she couldn't bring herself to snoop, not after he

had been so kind. Not after the misunderstanding about the iPod.

She logged on and immediately any worries concerning Tristan and Kenan vanished when she saw there were no messages from Jess.

Summer slumped back, hurt, and stared ahead of her.

She had planned to say so much to her old friend. Now everything she had wanted to write rang false. Why would Jess be interested? Summer could hear her friend's teasing voice now: 'Yeah right, so it must be *such a drag* living in a massive house with acres of garden and a beach you can walk to, and a fit guy with blond hair and dazzling eyes who just *happens* to turn up out of the blue. Look at me – my heart's *bleeding*.'

She thought, with mounting sadness, about how Jess and the place that had been home had, in such a short space of time, begun to take on an unreal quality. She squeezed her eyes shut, trying to remember it, but could only bring to mind flickering images, as though watching a tired old black-and-white film. Her memories had become static, fading and slipping through her grasp, falling out of reach. She had to make an effort to piece together Jess's features.

There was a dragging sensation in her chest, similar to the feeling she had had when she sat looking at her mother's coffin, as she understood the finality; knowing that her mother would never see the world again and that she, Summer, would never be able to talk to her or touch her ever again.

Now she would most probably never see Jess again either.

Summer's new life was here, at Bosleven. And she was nobody here. Sure, Tristan was trying to make her feel at home. But it was not her home. She had no friends here, no real family. She was a ghost in this house, in the garden, on the cliffs, on the beach. A shadow. Everything was thin, insubstantial; none of it meant anything to her. She would never own her bedroom here as she had back in London. She could walk away that very day and she would not have left even the merest imprint on her new surroundings. No one would miss her.

She told herself to stop dwelling on such negative thoughts.

Write something. Anything. She must have been too busy. You'll have to make the first move.

She looked up at the screen and began to type.

Hey, Jess! Finally I get to a computer. You won't believe half of what I'm going to tell you. And the worse thing is, I still haven't got a phone. And even if I had, they say mobiles don't work here . . .

She tried her best to describe Bosleven, Tristan, Kenan. She didn't mention the beach. Or Zach. It was as though

117

she needed to keep something for herself.

Her finger hovered over the 'send' button, then she pressed 'delete' instead.

What was the point?

She had her hand behind the screen, about to close the laptop, when she heard someone come into the room behind her. She turned to look over her shoulder, expecting Tristan with a mug of tea.

'He told me I had to come up.'

It was Kenan. He had tea with him.

'Here.' He all but threw the drink at her.

'Careful!' she cried, as hot liquid splashed across her hand, narrowly missing the keyboard.

'No, *you* be careful,' said Kenan, leaning in close. 'You be very careful, *Summer*. This is my home, do you get it? I don't know why you're here or why the moment you arrive my mum takes herself off, but I'm going to find out and when I do, you'll wish you'd never set foot in Bosleven.'

Summer made to push him away when they were both startled by a shout from down below in the hallway.

'Don't *touch* me, Triss!' The voice was shrill.

Kenan's mouth dropped open. He froze for a second and the look on his face sent a ripple of panic through Summer.

'Mum . . .' he whispered.

He looks like he's seen a ghost now. Or heard one.

118

Kenan had lost his intent look of menace. His face was washed with shock, his eyes wide. He was instantly a little boy again, lost and startled like an animal, caught in the headlights of a vehicle on a dark road.

Summer too was held in the moment as the adult voices carried up the stairs.

'No! I'm not going to accept it! I've told you why. You *know* why!'

Summer saw Kenan react physically to what he had heard, as though he had been slapped in the face. Then he sprang to life, pushing past her, yelling, 'Out of my way!'

Summer stayed in the study, her breathing shallow, listening to Kenan's footsteps hammering down the stairs.

Tristan's voice came next, a series of low, gentle murmurings. She couldn't hear what he was saying.

She edged along the landing, an intruder, checking over her shoulder in case Kenan was nearby. She went only as far as the banister, fearing any sound which might draw attention to her presence. She need not have worried; a riot of smashing crockery ricocheted from the kitchen into the hall and up the stairwell. A scream ripped through the house.

Summer's hands fluttered to her throat, but still she moved forward, unable to help herself.

'I can't stand it! You're so calm! So measured! You

think *I* should be? Well, I'm not!' The woman. Her aunt. Hysterical. 'I've tried, God knows I've tried, to get my head around this. I can't do it. I don't owe her anything. *You* don't owe her anything. She made her feelings clear, Triss! She's got to go.'

'Please!' Tristan's voice now, raised and agitated.

Before she could check herself, ask herself whether she should intervene, Summer was racing down the stairs towards the row.

She had got halfway when there was an angry shout from behind.

'DON'T!'

She teetered and leaned on the banister to stop herself from falling as she looked up.

'How did you—?' she gasped. 'I heard you go downstairs. Where have you been hiding?'

Kenan lurched down to her and grabbed her arm. 'Leave them alone.'

She thought for a second that he was going to hit her with his free hand. Instead he dug his fingers into the bare flesh of her arm and twisted it, wrenching her close to him.

'Don't go anywhere near her.' His voice fizzed with hatred. His face was close to hers, spit flying on to her cheek.

She instinctively remained still. The voices in the kitchen had stopped. With unmistakable finality the

120

sound of a slammed door crashed through the house. With that, Kenan changed from a young man full of rage to a lost child.

'Mum!' He hurtled down the stairs and out of the house after his mother, chasing her car's screeching departure down the gravel drive.

Summer waited until she was sure Kenan was not coming back, and sank to her knees.

She didn't know how long she stayed there, on the cool dark stairs. She listened as sounds of normality returned to the kitchen. The clink of crockery in the sink, the cascade of taps running into the plastic bowl for the washing-up.

'*Miaooow.*'

'Oh!' Summer flinched. 'You do like to startle me, don't you?'

The little white cat jumped lightly on to her lap, purring as loudly as ever. It curled into a ball, wrapping its tail neatly around itself and seemed to go to sleep.

Summer hugged the small creature to her, grateful for the comfort of its warmth. She turned over in her mind the words she had heard. Something her aunt had said did not make sense. What had she meant by saying, 'She made her feelings clear'? Becca hadn't meant *her*, Summer: they had not yet set eyes on one another. So who had made their feelings clear?

Maybe the row was nothing to do with me.

121

Even as she had that thought, she knew it was wrong: Kenan was mad at her, his mum was upset. The two things must be linked.

Summer felt guilt twist her insides. How would she face Tristan after overhearing that row?

I didn't ask to be here. It's not my fault!

She remained on the step, paralysed with not knowing where to go, what to do.

Tristan appeared in the hallway. He moved as though he were carrying an ache deep inside him. His eyes widened when he glanced up and saw Summer.

He'll know I heard it all now.

'Summer – I . . . I'm so sorry.'

The cat reacted to his voice and leaped off Summer's lap, scurrying up the stairs into the shadows.

'Are you OK?'

What does he expect me to say after that row? He must know I heard it.

'I should have come up to check on you, I'm sorry about – but then Becca—' His voice cracked. He looked away briefly. 'You heard, I suppose?'

Summer couldn't speak.

Tristan gestured with his head to the kitchen, 'Want to come down?'

Summer fought the urge to turn and hide in her room, and did as Tristan said, following him. She felt certain she knew what would happen next.

He's going to chuck me out. They can't handle this. His wife won't come back until I'm gone. Well, it's what I wanted really. Isn't it?

She tried to harden herself against the anxiety swirling inside her. If he chucked her out where would she go? Not back to Jess's. She would be a cuckoo in that little nest as well.

'You heard the shouting,' Tristan was saying. 'The smashing plate too, no doubt. My wife, Becca . . . she . . . You'd guessed maybe already. She is not happy with you being here. I'm so sorry.' He gave a sigh. 'At least now you know why.'

'No, I *don't*!' Summer exploded, fear making her desperate.

'She doesn't want you here,' Tristan said quietly. 'There's no point in lying to you. She didn't want us to take you in after Cat died. We argued and I refused to turn you away. How could I? How could anyone?'

The words hit her with such force that Summer put her hand to her cheek.

'She doesn't want you here.'

Her head spun. What was he saying? That he cared enough about her to keep her in his house, even if it meant his wife leaving him? That he wasn't blaming her for this? She sat down hard, on a kitchen chair.

'Why?' she whispered. 'Why doesn't she want me here?'

Tristan shook his head. He would not look her in the eye.

'Summer, I'm sorry. I can't tell you right now. I'm . . . I'm upset. I only wanted to reassure you, in case you were worried, that this is your home and I am not going to abandon you.'

Why? Why? WHY?

'I can't . . . We will have to talk about this later. I need to think things through. Maybe you should get some fresh air.' He ran a hand through his hair.

'Yes,' she said quietly. 'I will.'

To the sea. To breathe.

'See you later.' She turned away.

Tristan nodded. 'Yes. I . . . I'm sorry,' he said again, his voice like the echo in an empty shell.

Chapter Thirteen

Summer found herself thinking about Zach as she made her way slowly through the rockery and out into the woods.

Stupid. You don't know him. And you shouted at him. Anyway, he won't still be there.

She broke into a run.

She had never *wanted* to run before coming to Bosleven. Sports at school had always been an exercise in humiliation. It was different here. She wanted to be outside, yearned for the air, the light, the freedom, the space.

She ran until she reached the clifftop, pushed through the brambles hiding the path to the beach, and then stopped, looking down at the bay.

Zach.

He was standing on the furthest point of the rocky beach, perfectly still, focused on his fishing line, rapt with concentration. The light bounced off the water before him. It was like a painting. Summer felt she shouldn't move, in case she spoilt the effect.

Then, as she watched him, Zach began reeling in the line with quick flicking movements of his wrist, until – yes! There was a fish wriggling on the end. He unhooked it and dropped it into a bucket by his side.

Summer felt a rush of pleasure at his success. 'Hey!' she called out without thinking.

Zach looked up, frowning into the light, then waved and grinned when he saw her. Encouraged, Summer began climbing over the boulders towards him.

He was fixing a new worm to the end of the line.

'Hey! So couldn't stay away then?' he teased.

Summer felt warmth spread through her and automatically dipped her face to hide her emotions as she approached.

She kept her voice casual. 'Yeah, well. It's better down here than back ho— up at the house. Water's really high now,' she went on, avoiding his eyes until she could trust herself not to blush again.

'Yeah. This is the highest it gets. About seven metres today. It'll be great for swimming – you bring your stuff again?'

'Hmm. Thought I'd just paddle.'

'Here,' he said, suddenly handing her the fishing rod, 'take this for a second. Ever done any fishing before?'

Summer laughed and shook her head. 'No way!'

'You can't come here and not fish!' he said. 'I'll show

you.' He demonstrated how to cast the line using a long, flowing, smooth motion. 'You try.'

Summer took the rod and tried to copy him. She threw the line forward and it whipped back against her, catching on her clothing. She did not have the grace that he had. She tried again with the same result.

Zach laughed. Then said, 'Sorry,' as he saw her unease.

She shrugged and handed the equipment back. 'I'll just watch.'

Zach prepared to cast the line again. 'Stand clear,' he warned.

The sunlight caught the line as it arced through the air; it seemed a natural extension of his brown arms.

Beautiful.

'Easy, see?' Zach said, turning to face her.

She raised her eyebrows. 'For you, maybe. What are you catching?'

'Mackerel. Sea bass, if I'm lucky. Can sell it for a good price. Mostly I eat the catch myself. Best thing is to gut it straight away, build a fire in a sheltered spot down here and cook it fresh from the water.' He spoke with relish, as though already tasting it. 'So,' he said, changing tack, 'did you tell your family?'

Summer started. 'What?'

'About this place,' Zach said. He looked worried.

'Family'? Ha! If only you knew.

'No,' she said.

'Oh dear. Hacked off with them again already?' he said.

'Erm . . . oh, I dunno,' Summer mumbled.

She felt confused and sank down, cross-legged, her face buried in her hands.

'Hey, hey!' Zach dropped his fishing rod with a clatter and crouched in front of her. 'What's up?'

She couldn't bear to look at him, fearing that the tears would well up again.

I mustn't cry. Mustn't. Not in front of him.

He placed a cool hand on her arm. 'Can't be that bad, can it? Might help to talk?'

Zach's words and touch made Summer tingle.

This guy's not for real!

She stayed hidden behind her curtain of hair and said, 'Don't think so.'

'My gran always says a problem shared is a problem halved,' Zach said softly.

When she did not reply, he rearranged himself to sit more comfortably alongside her. They sat in silence for a while. Summer began to relax as it became clear that Zach was not going to push it.

He simply sat, looking out across the bay to where the edge of the cliff path unravelled into the ragged rocks on the peninsula. He had a wistful half-smile on his face, as though he had forgotten she was there. A gentle breeze played with the fringes of his hair against his smooth cheeks.

Summer felt in that instant that she was outside herself, watching the pair of them: a boy and a girl, sitting on the rocks, completely content in one another's company as if they had known each other forever. Her mother's face swam before her eyes.

Were you here? With someone?

Summer made herself concentrate on the rocks beneath her, willing herself back to the present.

Must act normal.

Zach broke the silence. 'Listen, if it makes you feel better, I'll tell you a bit about myself,' he said. 'I'm Zachary Pendred, but I prefer "Zach". I live in the village – St Gerran – with my gran. Dad was a fisherman, died in an accident at sea. Mum . . . she couldn't cope. So now it's just me and Gran. I'm fourteen. I like fishing, the sea—'

'You sound like you're applying for a job!' Summer's voice was hoarse from crying.

What did I say that for?

Zach shifted. 'Yeah, well, maybe I am – job of new friend?'

'Don't bother,' Summer heard herself say. 'I'm not sticking around.'

Why do I have to be such a cow?

She began to get up. It was best she left.

But Zach put his hand out and touched her arm again to stop her from going.

'Sorry,' she said. She sat back down and looked at her scuffed trainers. 'You're being really nice and I'm being horrible.'

''S all right. Listen, I'm going to carry on fishing. If you want to stay, stay. If you want to talk, fine. If not . . . whatever.' He reached over to reclaim his abandoned line and began fiddling with it, then stood up and took himself back to where he had been when she arrived.

Summer let her head fall back and stared emptily at the vast pale blue sky.

Just talk to him.

Licking her lips, she took a deep breath and rattled off her own sparse CV: 'So. I'm Summer Jones. My mum's dead, I've never had a dad, and I'm living with my uncle who's weird and my cousin who's a jerk and who wishes I was dead too. Oh, and my aunt's mad at me – wishes I'd never been born, apparently.'

This harsh voice did not belong to her.

Zach reeled in the line. He nodded slowly, but still didn't speak.

Summer grimaced. 'Right little sob story, eh?'

'Got a couple of things in common with me, I guess.' Zach shrugged.

'Maybe. 'Cept you didn't say your gran was a nightmare?'

'No. She's not,' Zach said with a smile.

'And so far no one is mad at you or thinks you're a jerk?'

Zach held her gaze. 'Hope not.'

Summer flushed, pushed at her messy hair and got up. She wished she could plunge into the sea, however cold it was, and let the water close over her and hide her appearance. The large arch of rock across the bay looked back at her, ancient and knowing.

'That's the Point,' Zach said, following her gaze. 'You can fish from there too – if you can climb it.'

'Have you?' Summer asked. She stole a small glance at him.

He smiled, his nose wrinkling. 'Yeah. I'll take you there. If you like.'

'Not *now*?' Scrambling down the cliff the short way to this beach was all very well; but climbing up a steep rock face like that? She did not know if she could.

'No!' Zach laughed. 'There's no time today: I've got to get back soon. It's a half-day trip from my place to the Point if I want to fish as well. Another day?'

Summer felt a rush of pleasure at the offer.

'You can swim over there on a day as calm as this,' Zach continued. 'Then do a rock climb back. Maybe light a fire after – if you can find enough driftwood.'

'You love this place,' Summer said. She immediately felt stupid. The words had slipped out.

'It's the best place in the world.'

'Do you . . . do you come here a lot?'

Zach nodded. 'Much as I can. All year round as well. Of course it's different in the winter. Crashing waves, howling winds. Romantic, I guess – if you like that sort of thing!' he said. Then hastily, 'I'm not supposed to come here, though. Definitely not to fish. You won't tell, will you? It's a private beach, you see. Belongs to a big house up there.' He waved in the direction of Bosleven. 'They don't like people coming down here.'

Summer knew she would have to keep quiet about Tristan and Kenan now.

He was still talking. 'There's loads of other beaches and coves, of course. There's Lamorna. You can walk there from here . . .'

Lamorna?

'What did you say?'

'Lamorna,' Zach repeated. 'What's up? Know the place, do you?'

'I – no. No, I don't.'

Summer Lamorna Jones.

She had always hated that middle name. Just too weird. Was it a clue? Her mother could not have chosen the name by chance, any more than she could have sent Summer to Bosleven on a whim.

I'm not going to tell him. He wouldn't believe me. I could ask Tristan. If he ever lets me ask him anything again.

She pushed away thoughts of her uncle and what was waiting for her back at the house. 'So. Might see you tomorrow then?' she said casually.

Zach reeled in his line. Nothing on the end this time. 'Yeah,' he said. He began dismantling his fishing rod, then bobbed down into a crouch and concentrated on packing away the tackle. 'I'll be here. First thing probably.' He looked up. 'Be good if you were too.'

'Yeah,' she said. She turned abruptly and began skipping over the rocks back to the cliffs. 'See you!'

Chapter Fourteen

The next morning, Tristan was already in his study when Summer emerged. He barely looked up from his desk when she knocked on the door to say good morning. She had glanced into Kenan's room too. The door had been open, the curtains thrown wide; it seemed as though he had not been there overnight. He must have caught up with his mother after all.

Nevertheless, Summer made her way down the stairs cautiously, just in case he was waiting to have another go at her.

I need to talk to Tristan about Mum.

Outside the window an ominous black bank of cloud rolled in from the sea, cloaking the tall pines and the side path in darkness.

She wondered if Zach would be likely to go to the rocks anyway, seeing as they had made an arrangement to meet.

Yeah, like he's going to sit in the rain, waiting for me.

The clouds finally broke over the garden and fat raindrops hit the windows. She had absolutely no idea what to do with herself.

She went back to her room, riffled through the books she had brought. None of them were new to her, though, and she did not feel like re-reading anything. Then she considered the bookcase outside her bedroom door.

She went to see if there was anything worth reading there. She remembered how, yesterday, she had thought somebody had knocked some of the books from the shelves, and shuddered now as she ran her fingers over the worn spines.

Around the World in Eighty Days. The War of the Worlds. The Black Tulip.

The books were ancient. They must have seen a thing or two in their time. Summer focused on the titles, sternly telling herself not to think spooky thoughts. She picked up a book and flicked through the musty, thin pages. She was about to take it back to her room when she heard a noise on the other side of the bookcase. A scraping noise, as though someone were running their fingernails down the wood behind the books.

She stumbled back, away from the shelves, her heart thumping. Then there was a sharp knocking noise: the books wobbled on the shelves and someone – a woman? – laughed. A deep, throaty laugh which sounded all too familiar.

Summer dropped the book as she let out a scream and ran back to her room.

Slamming the door behind her, she leaned against it, her eyes closed. Her body was seized with panic.

It was not Mum. It was nothing. There is no such thing as ghosts.

She tried to calm herself, but there was no getting away from what she had just heard. No making sense of it either.

When she opened her eyes, she saw that the cat was sitting on her bed, flicking its tail and observing her coolly.

'For flip's sake, cat!' she scolded. 'I've already had one heart attack – what are you trying to do to me?'

She bent over to pick up the cat, suddenly desperate to feel a real, live creature, to bring herself back down to earth.

But the cat did not want a cuddle; it slithered from her grasp, its body liquid. It made for the door and scratched at it, mewing pitifully to be let out.

Summer shook her head. 'I'm not opening that door,' she said.

The cat was insistent, its mewing increasingly loud.

'OK, OK.'

She relented and shakily opened the door, ready to slam it closed behind the animal, but it whisked round and sat right in the opening, preventing Summer from shutting it out, looking back at her pointedly.

'You want me to come with you?'

She remembered how the cat had led her to the beach. Then admonished herself.

Cats do not lead people anywhere. It's your imagination again.

She made a move towards the cat to shoo it away. It budged slightly, and then sat and waited for her again. She sighed. The cat was trying to tell her something.

'Are you hungry?'

'*Miiaooow!*' It sounded as though it were telling her off for not understanding.

'I do not want to leave this room,' she said.

She considered pushing the cat roughly aside, but something in her needed to know what the animal wanted. So she stepped over the creature, avoiding looking at the bookcase, and waited. The cat gave a small, chirruping purr as though to say 'At last!' and trotted past her, then stopped once more, checking to see if she was going to follow.

'I'm coming, I'm coming,' she muttered, secretly relieved to have the company, even if it was only the company of a cat.

The animal scampered along the landing with Summer close behind, then instead of going down, as Summer had supposed it would, it veered up the stairs Tristan had said led to the attic.

Summer stopped short.

No way am I going up into any scary attic!

The thought of cobwebs and shadowy corners was enough to make her freeze at the foot of the stairs. She felt she had to make sure that no one was watching her: the thought of that laughter from behind the bookcase made her shudder. But as she listened for any sign of more unexplained noises, she found the place was now so quiet that all she could hear was the house itself, clicking and crackling around her.

She was cross with herself for being so pathetic: ghosts in the attic? How clichéd and childish. In any case, Kenan had not told her any stories about ghosts in the attic: he had said they were in the servants' quarters.

The cat had stopped outside a door at the top of the stairs and was mewing again.

'You'd better not be about to play a trick on me.' Summer spoke out loud, feeling foolish, but needing to hear her own voice.

She pushed open the door and emerged into a light, airy, open-plan space – not dark and dank and full of boxes, her idea of what an attic should be. On the contrary, this was one long big room in the eaves with two small fire grates, one at either end. Had this been divided into bedrooms too at one time? Curiosity was already overcoming fear as Summer began to look around.

Discarded belongings lay strewn about the floor. There was as much stuff up here as in those rooms in the kitchen passage. For a small family, the Trewarthas had accumulated a lot of junk.

She picked her way through piles of old clothing, heaps of papers, tottering towers of books. The cat was sitting on a small pile of them – old-fashioned, cloth-bound, like the ones in the bookcase outside Summer's room. She bent to scoop it up, half expecting it to struggle out of her grasp as it had done before. Its skinny body went limp when she put her hands around its middle, however, and as she lifted it to her chest, it settled against her and began a deep, contented, rhythmical purr that resonated through her, comforting her.

On the far wall there was some shelving, all of it crammed with more books and folders and more paperwork. Just as in Tristan's study, it looked as though someone had broken in and gone through the lot in a tearing hurry to find what they were looking for.

Not that there could have been anything of any worth or interest here. She picked up a yellowing piece of lacy material. Dust rose out of it in billows and the fabric disintegrated under her fingers.

The cat hissed suddenly and slithered out of her arms, lightly bounding over the jumble on the floor and skittering excitedly after something.

Summer climbed over the junk, calling softly for the cat, which had vanished into the chaos. She bashed her shin against a toy pram with one wheel missing. It was heaped with the contorted bodies of abandoned dolls and teddies, as if caught in a bomb blast and hurled from their homes. One doll in particular had a haunting face; an eye missing, its hair tangled, a hand thrown up to shield itself from an unseen enemy.

A large cushion lay half submerged beneath scattered papers. Summer heaved at it and freed it from the clutches of a box of old files and a child's broken tricycle. It was dusty, of course, and bursting at the seams where some yellow and green foamy stuffing poked out, but it would make a good seat. Summer cleared a space around it, then gingerly sat down, shuffling into the cushion as it responded to her shape.

'Miaoooowweeeeeeeee!'

The cat appeared from somewhere to her left and soared through the air as though it had been singed, its fur electrified, its eyes and mouth stretched wide.

Summer scrambled to her feet and looked around to see what had frightened the cat.

Nothing. Not even the faintest rustle.

She was about to settle herself back on to the cushion, silently cursing the cat, when she saw that a tin box next to her was shedding its contents, its lid on askew.

Photos.

The images were faded and most of them were fuzzy, badly focused. The colours were overexposed, but one element leaped from the frame: the people's faces.

Summer stared at the pictures, blinking, disbelieving.

No, I'm – I'm not seeing straight. It's my mind playing tricks . . . Why do I keep seeing her?

The photographs had been taken on the beach where Summer had been with Zach. She recognized the shape of the arch of craggy rocks in the distance across the bay. She recognized something else too.

Her mum in a bathing costume, sitting where Summer had sat as she gazed out to sea. Except that her mum was gazing at something else – or rather some*one* else. She was staring directly at the person taking the photo. She was so young. And so happy. Summer felt it was like looking at pictures of herself as she had felt when she had first found the rocks. A happy, free, beautiful version of herself.

Summer took a handful of photos from the top of the box and shuffled through them: photo after photo of her mum. They were all taken right there, at Bosleven. There was the lawn, the old driveway behind her mother, the house, and then the beach. Her mum looked so fresh, so pretty, her dark hair mussed up in the sea breeze, her skirts shorter than she would ever have allowed Summer to wear, her long legs tanned. And so healthy. Not like the fragile shadow of a mother she had been the last time Summer had seen her.

What does this mean?

When she had tried to work out her relationship to the Trewarthas, she had asked if her mother was related to them. Tristan had not given a satisfactory response, saying only that he was 'a *distant* uncle'. Judging from the photos, Catherine had been to Bosleven many times in the past. And if Bosleven had belonged to Becca's family before she and Tristan had moved in, Catherine must have known Becca quite well. They must have been close once . . . Were they cousins or something?

So maybe Becca is not angry with me at all. Is she angry with Mum?

Should she search through all the junk in the attic for more clues? She carefully put the photos back into the tin and pressed the lid down firmly. She wanted to take the box with her, keep it in her room and look through it thoroughly later. Perhaps she could show it to Tristan and demand some answers.

'*Miaaoooow!*' The cat jumped out from behind the pram and landed on her, sinking his claws into her thighs.

'For goodness sake, cat!' she yelled, jumping up and dropping the tin. Her sudden movement sent the pram flying, the dolls falling out on top of the chaos around her, burying the tin amongst so much paper and junk. 'What's the matter with you?' she cried, kicking at the mess in front of her.

'*Miaow!*' the cat protested. Then it hissed and ran away.

Summer surveyed the scene before her and suddenly

felt overwhelmed – by the piles of stuff and her jumbled feelings.

Those photographs had made her realize that she knew nothing about herself: she had always thought she knew who she was – Summer Jones, daughter of Catherine – and what her life would be – a life in London with Jess as her best mate, doing everything together, growing up together.

Not any more.

She could not rely on anyone to be straight with her, to tell her the truth or look after her. She had only herself.

She bent to retrieve the tin, but stopped. She could not take it to Tristan: she would have to admit to going through his possessions. The way he was at the moment, who knew how he might react to that?

If I come out with it and ask him about Mum being here, he'll have to give me some answers. But if he's angry with me for searching through stuff . . .

She called for the cat, which had disappeared again.

'Here, puss-puss-puss—!'

'What do you think you are doing?'

She whirled round.

Kenan was standing in the doorway. He laughed nastily. 'Having a good old poke around, are you?'

'No, I—'

'First you split my mum and dad up and now you go snooping through our things. You're wasting your time.

You won't find the family silver up here,' he scoffed.

Summer fumed. 'I am not looking for anything like that. And I have not split anyone up!'

'Yeah, right. Must be the world record for splitting up a family – what's it been? Less than a week. So what's the next step? Moving into my room? Kicking us all out, maybe?'

Summer was stiff with anger. 'Who do you think you are, Mummy's boy?'

A vein was throbbing on his scrawny white neck, spots of red had appeared on his cheeks.

He threw himself at her, grabbed her and shoved her to the ground. He stood over her, his eyes flashing. 'You – shut – up!' he said through clenched teeth. 'Mum is finding a way of getting rid of you, and when she has, you'll have to go.'

She held her breath, waiting for him to finish what he had started, convinced he would hit her, hurt her.

Go on, now's your chance.

Instead he glared at her for a beat longer, making sure she had got his message loud and clear, then he stood back, turned and ran down the stairs, only letting out a sob once he was out of range.

Summer heard him slam his door. She lay on the attic floor, knowing she would have to spend the rest of the day in her room if she was going to avoid Kenan's fury.

There was nowhere else to go.

Chapter Fifteen

The next morning the weather was good enough to venture down to the rocks.

Summer could not wait to get out of the house. Even the thought of going back for a second look at those photos was not enough to keep her inside, not while Kenan was around. She knew she should feel some sympathy; that he was as upset and confused as she was. That argument between his mum and dad had let something loose in the family and Kenan was determined to take it out on her. Try as she might, though, she could not feel anything but hatred for the boy; not after he had threatened her.

So she turned down the chance of a trip into Penzance with her uncle when he said Kenan would be coming too.

Summer waited until they had gone down the long gravel drive, then hurriedly crammed her swimming stuff into a rolled-up towel and set off. As she went, she tried to piece together the few clues that she had about her mum's decision to send her to Bosleven if anything ever happened to her.

Her mother had definitely been here – those photos

in the attic could not lie – so why had it never come up in conversation? Then there was Summer's own middle name, Lamorna: a local place.

Summer would never have admitted it to anyone, but in spite of her worries and fears, she felt these ties bound her to Bosleven now. However much she hated Kenan, and however frustrated she was with his father, the place had got under her skin. Especially now she knew for sure that her mother had loved it here – the look on her face in those photos demonstrated how happy she had been, at least on the beach. Summer could understand that: she had felt the same way the minute she pushed through the brambles and saw the cove beneath her.

The house still spooked her, though; whatever Tristan had said about old houses creaking and shifting, she was not reassured.

But the beach – she already thought of the beach as hers.

I belong here. Mum thought so. I just have to find out why.

She walked along the path Kenan had told her was haunted, and remembered the laugh behind the bookcase and the other strange noises she had heard in the house; remembered Kenan talking about the ghosts of old servants.

I can't let him freak me out.

She still felt uneasy. What had caused the books to

wobble on the shelves? Who had been laughing?

She looked up to where there was a gap in the shrubs and trees. There were dilapidated stone steps set into the wall, which itself was crumbling, eaten into by ivy and ferns. The steps led up to a tiny, flattened area which served as a small terrace, and a larger bit of crumbled rock served as a seat.

A look-out.

Summer picked her way over nettles and thorns to the steps, climbed up and sat on the stone bench. There was a perfect view of the sea from there. She wondered if Zach was waiting – if he had been waiting for her yesterday, in spite of the rain. She drew her legs up and hugged her knees, squashed her back flat against the wall and faced the house.

Can anyone see me from the kitchen?

She didn't think she was visible in this dark corner. She felt safe. Just as she had at the beach that first time – before Zach had turned up.

She shuffled round so that she was facing the sea again, the house behind her, closed her eyes and made herself listen to the soothing background music of the sea.

If she concentrated, the sounds that filled her head reminded her of the kind of thing Mum had listened to on the radio. There was the wind, softly sounding like the strings in an orchestra; there were the birds, fluting the melody. She smiled to herself. A gull cried out, its infant bawling breaking through the gentleness of the other noises around her.

What instrument would that be? A trumpet? One of those wooden squeaky things, maybe . . . What were they called? Oboe, that's it.

That is when she heard another instrument, faint and rippling. It gradually became more insistent, drawing Summer out of her thoughts, demanding her attention.

No, you're hearing things.

The music crescendoed. A piano. The notes coming faster, stronger, urgently carrying across the lawn through an open window.

Not possible. Tristan had told her that he didn't have 'a musical bone' in him. Anyway, he had gone with Kenan — surely they weren't back already? She hadn't been out in the garden that long. She looked at her wrist and saw with irritation that she wasn't wearing her watch.

Whoever was playing knew what they were doing. This was not someone mucking around out of curiosity: they were playing with obvious skill. Vast cascading scales of notes were growing, swelling; chords chimed out sonorous bass notes while a higher, lighter trickle of melody ran down over the top, like the stream in the rockery pouring over the granite beneath. The music carried clear and bright through the hot, still air.

Tristan's wife? He said she played. Surely not? She's not here . . .

If her aunt was there, Summer had no desire to meet her on her own. The woman clearly despised her. What would she say?

Yet she was drawn irresistibly by the sound. Hearing that music and thinking of the sea, the two things seemed combined, as if the sea were creating the music, or the music were painting the scene before her. She had to get closer, to see who could be playing like that. Even if it was her aunt.

She checked herself. Was she ready to meet this person who 'did not want her here'?

The music made up her mind for her. Summer left the bench and turned on to the path, taking a decisive step towards the house. She used the cover of the trees to shield her from the house in case Kenan had come back early, making her way along the path until she was at the closest point to the room with the piano in it. The 'drawing room', Tristan had called it.

She reached the house and edged her way along to the French windows, keeping close to the rough, grey walls. Then she turned her head and glanced quickly through the glass into the shady room.

The music immediately seemed to bloom, to become crystal clear and vivid. It had lost the floating quality it had had from a distance and was now more insistent, the rippling arpeggios compelling Summer to lean in and peer through the window.

Who is it?

She couldn't see clearly. She pressed her face closer to the glass.

A woman, definitely a woman. But not a stranger. The curve of those shoulders, the shape of the neck, the colour of the hair were all too familiar. Even from the back she knew who it was.

'No!' she shouted aloud and stumbled back.

The noise she made startled the woman at the piano. She stopped playing and turned to look out of the window.

Summer felt the blood drain from her face.

It is! It's Mum!

The figure quickly got up from the piano stool to make her way to the window. She was mouthing something.

It was too much. With a sob, Summer turned and ran. She ran and ran without stopping or thinking until she had reached the rockery. She pushed through the hydrangeas. She only stopped when her lungs began to burn, her legs heavy and useless. She listened, straining for the sounds of anyone following her.

But I wouldn't hear *a ghost's footsteps, would I?*

Fear pushed her on. She did not stop this time until she had reached the cliff edge.

Chapter Sixteen

Summer, now in her swimming things, had been sitting for a while, her feet dangling in the cold water of the pool cut from the rock.

Where do I fit into all this?

'Go on. Take a dip!'

She whirled round in fright.

She hasn't come down?

It was only Zach, standing behind her, silhouetted against the afternoon sun. He too was in his swimming trunks, and he was laughing at her.

'You numpty! You scared me.'

'Sorry.' He looked sheepish. 'So. Where were you yesterday?'

'You weren't here? In *that* rain?' she said. She watched herself slip into this easy banter.

Look at me, chatting away. Like I haven't just seen my mother's ghost . . .

'Course. Rain never lasts too long – not in the summer. 'S always worth waiting for it to pass. I sheltered in the cave. It didn't rain *all* day, you know. Not hard anyway.'

His smile wrapped itself around her. 'So are we going for a swim or what, then? Go on!' he urged when she started to protest. 'I promise I won't let anything happen to you.'

'It's not that – it's just so cold,' Summer said. She burned with shame, wanting to be tougher than this. She should be tougher than this.

'It'll be good for you!' Zach insisted. 'You'll get used to the cold. It's best to jump right in. Like this.' He held his nose and took a running leap out into the bay.

She held her breath until she saw Zach coming up for air. Then his head burst through the glassy skin of water, his eyes closed, his cheeks puffed out, his hair slick against his scalp. He shook his head like a playful dog, sending spray in all directions, and blew out noisily through his nose and mouth.

'Hey, it's amazing!' he yelled, letting out a raucous bellow of laughter. His eyes were still tight shut, the jewel-drop splashes around him flashing like diamonds. He looked as though he were born to be there: a sea creature, a mer-boy. Truly in his element.

Zach swam closer to where she was still sitting awkwardly on the edge. 'Come on, Summer!' he pressed.

When she didn't say anything, he formed a shovel with his cupped hands and pushed a wall of water at her, soaking her legs and body, sending up a shower of sparkling, icy water into her face.

'Urgh!' she shouted, scrabbling to her feet.

'Now that you're wet, you may as well get in,' he teased, his head on one side. His smile was softer now, his eyes betraying a flicker of worry; perhaps he had gone too far.

Summer's mouth twitched with mischief, and suddenly, recklessly, she threw herself straight at him, wanting to feel alive and carefree, to have some fun. She momentarily enjoyed the look of shock on his face as she fell towards him, then realized, too late, what she was doing.

I'm jumping into the water – it's freezing!

Zach had already grabbed her arm before she could sink too deep. She surfaced, spluttering, her legs and free arm flapping and struggling.

'It's OK, it's OK, I've got you,' Zach said. His face was very close to hers, his grip on her surprisingly strong.

Gradually the tightness around her chest eased, the iron-clad cold loosening its grasp. A fuzzy feeling of almost-warmth crept into her limbs as her blood raced around her veins.

'See? Not so bad, is it?' said Zach's voice in her ear. 'Once you're used to the cold, you'll find it easier than swimming in a pool.'

'Hm-hmm,' she said, through pursed lips. Summer didn't dare talk. She didn't want to let any more of the sharp, salty water into her mouth.

'OK,' said Zach carefully. 'I won't take you out into the bay, even though it's a lovely calm day. We'll stay here in this smaller area – I call this bit the Pool. Whatever's going on beyond the rocks, the Pool mostly always stays calm. We'll be completely safe. You all right now?'

'Uh-huh.' Summer nodded.

Zach let go of her and propelled himself round, sculling with his hands in small circles. 'See the way the Pool is sheltered by the line of the rocks around it? The water hardly ever gets that rough in the summer. Out in the bay, it can get choppy. Still, you'll have to try it. That's where the real swimming is!'

She had to admit, it was wonderful: quiet, soft water that she could have sworn had gone up a fair few degrees in temperature since she had taken the plunge, the only sounds a shallow dabbling as they both paddled idly. She closed her eyes for a second and smiled.

'Told you it was magic,' Zach said.

'Do you ever wonder where you come from?' Zach asked. They were sitting on the rocks, wrapped in their towels.

She looked at him sharply, her limbs shaking with cold now that the adrenaline had dissipated. 'N-n-no,' she said through shivering lips. Every hair on her arms was standing to attention.

Zach was looking out across the cove to the peninsula. *That's the rock in the background of those photos of mum. Should I tell him about them?*

The sun was behind Zach, giving him a golden halo. His cute nose wrinkled up as he smiled. His tanned skin looked darker, bathed in this light.

'I bet you do,' he said, and returned her gaze slowly. He seemed to look right into her.

'Bet I do what?'

'Wonder where you come from – You all right? You look a bit shaky,' he added.

''S all right,' she said, hugging her towel tightly around her. 'What you were saying – about where we come from? I . . . yeah, I s'pose I do.' She wasn't sure about being drawn into a conversation about her family. Yet at the same time, she was thinking of a way to mention Tristan and Kenan, even maybe those photos, without actually telling him she was living at Bosleven.

'I think about it a lot,' he said. 'I sometimes think: what if my parents had never met? Or if they'd met other people, I mean?' The blue of his eyes seemed to deepen as he leaned forward, intent. 'Would I have been born as a different person? Or would I still have been born, but just ended up in a different family? Or would I have been born a girl?' He chuckled at the thought.

Summer snorted. 'Idiot,' she said, teeth still chattering. She was smiling now, though.

She had never met anyone who talked like this. Even Jess. If ever Summer had tried anything approaching a philosophical conversation with her, Jess had only laughed and teased her for being 'deep'. Zach was so different. The contrast with him and Kenan, or any of the boys from school, was huge. She couldn't let him see this. Had to play it cool.

'Once I get to thinking like that,' Zach was saying, 'I go off on one, you know – like, I start thinking, what if this is all a dream?'

'Oh, that's original,' Summer said, teasing.

'No – I don't mean, "What if I'm dreaming it?",' Zach persisted. 'I mean, "What if someone *else* is dreaming all this?"' He looked up to the cliffs and the sky and motioned expansively, taking in their surroundings. 'What if this is someone else's dream, and we're just characters in it: if they wake up, what happens to us?'

'That's just mental, you know that?' Summer said, nudging him. She wanted to say she had already thought similar things herself, but could not bring herself to be as open as he was.

'By the way,' Zach said lightly, as if on cue, 'you still haven't told me that much about yourself yet . . .' he tailed off.

Summer sighed. He was right. He had done all the running so far: if they were going to be friends, she would have to tell him a bit more than she already had.

'I . . . if I tell you where I'm staying, will you promise not to freak out on me?' she said seriously.

Zach pulled a face. 'S'pose.'

'Sorry, I mean, that sounds weird, I guess, it's just – I didn't know this place was private till you told me yesterday. But you probably won't believe that when you hear . . . Oh, whatever, you'd find out sooner or later probably.' She blew at her salt-streaked hair and picked at some barnacles. 'I only came here very recently. After Mum died. My uncle's . . . I'm staying at that house.' She said the words quickly, before she could change her mind, and jerked her head up towards the cliffs. Couldn't bring herself to say, 'I *live* there'.

'What? Bosleven?' Zach's eyes popped wide with shock and surprise. He drew away slightly. 'You are kidding me, right?'

Summer shook her head. 'Nope. Tristan Trewartha's my guardian. He's supposed to be some kind of uncle. I never knew him before, though. I mean, Mum never told me about this place and then she died and . . . Well, I had to come here.'

'Right,' said Zach slowly.

Summer glanced at him anxiously.

'I'm not going to tell him about you fishing here or anything,' she assured him hastily.

'No,' said Zach.

'To be honest, I don't think they come down here that much.'

Zach smiled sadly.

157

Summer was anxious at this sudden clouding of his mood. 'Listen, if I knew it was going to upset you, knowing who my uncle is, I never would have told you.'

Zach shook his head. 'I know.' He stood up. 'Hey, I didn't realize your mum had died so recently. I'm . . . I'm sorry.'

'It's fine,' Summer muttered.

'Listen,' Zach said softly. 'I'm sorry I asked so many questions. If you don't want to talk about it, that's cool.'

Summer said nothing.

'What are you doing tomorrow?' Zach asked suddenly. 'Want to come on a bike ride?'

Summer looked up.

His face was shining with genuine excitement at his idea. 'I could show you the village – unless you've already been there. Or take you to another beach?'

Summer bit her lip. She had a suspicion he was only being nice to her now because of her mum, but she found she did not really care about the motivation behind his suggestion. They both spoke at once.

'I'd love to—

'It's OK, no worries. It was only a thought—'

'No, really,' she cut in. 'I'd love to explore. I – I don't know my way round yet, so . . .'

'Great! Do you have a bike? I could come and get you?'

'No,' she said. Then, quickly, 'I mean: I don't have a bike.'

Zach looked disappointed. 'Oh.' He chewed at a nail.

Summer churned with frustration. She had just had the offer of a chance to get out. The chance to spend time with someone she wanted to be with. Someone Kenan knew nothing about.

So near, yet so far.

Then Zach said, 'Hey, I bet they've got a bike. Up at the house. Must have. You could borrow one.'

She swallowed drily. 'What if – what if they find me poking around and . . . get cross?'

Zach frowned. 'Why would they do that? If that Tristan guy is your guardian, surely he won't mind if you borrow a bike, for heaven's sake?'

Summer's brow furrowed too. 'It's not him.'

Zach looked at her curiously. 'I'll walk back up with you now. I left my bike in a bush near the field with the pigs in – you know?'

She shook her head. She hadn't noticed any pigs.

'It's by the green gate – the one that goes into their rockery. You must have seen the rockery? It's famous round here. Famous for being a secret – like the beach!' He laughed.

Yeah. Like a lot of things.

Zach put a hand on her shoulder. 'OK, listen, when you go back now, see what you can do about a bike. I'll wait for you tomorrow at the top of their drive – ten o'clock? If you're not there by half past, I won't wait. But . . . I won't hold it against you.' He laughed. 'I'm always down here fishing anyway, so . . .'

'Yeah,' Summer replied softly.

They gathered their things and headed back up the cliff path, Zach chattering amiably about showing her round, and Summer half listening as she stole sideways looks at him.

Maybe there was more than one reason for not wanting to leave Bosleven now.

Chapter Seventeen

There *was* a bike. Summer had seen it on her wanderings through the kitchen passage. She knew it would be difficult to extract from the abandoned objects crowded in there, but she was determined to give it a go.

The moment she got back to the house she went straight to the room where she had remembered seeing it. Stepping with exaggerated care so as not to trip, she reached the bike and put her hands on the handlebars. The metal frame was rough. Rusty probably. Would it work?

She tugged at it and it yielded easily, rolling forward. *One, two, three . . .*

She lifted the bike off the ground. It was heavier than she had expected, but she managed to get it to chest height, her arms shaking with the effort as she stepped back to set the bike down.

It was not locked, she noted with relief. She was sure she had made a hell of a noise, clanking around in there, but a quick check assured her the house was quiet. She had decided to hide the bike somewhere so that she could get at it easily the next day without being heard.

She wheeled it into the passage, the tyres reassuringly bouncy on the terracotta tiles.

Once outside, she sized it up properly. It was ancient: thick-framed, black, with paint peeling off it in scratchy patches. There was a wicker basket slung on the handlebars. It was the sort of thing old lady detectives on TV used to cycle into the local village and solve a crime or two on a Sunday afternoon after taking tea with the vicar.

Summer wheeled the bike slowly to the drive. Tristan and Kenan were not back yet: the car was not there.

She decided to try the bike for size. Wobbling and cursing, she swerved from side to side, praying she would not end up falling into the hydrangeas. She got the hang of steering it quicker than she had thought possible, and felt a rush of exhilaration as she picked up speed, jolting along the drive.

Why hadn't she thought of this before? She could have got away days ago, gone for long cycle rides and explored further afield.

She was not going to let herself think negative thoughts now. She had something concrete to look forward to for the first time since coming to Bosleven. A day out. With Zach.

Zach arrived at ten the next day, as he said he would. She was waiting for him.

'Hey! Fantastic!' he called, freewheeling the last stretch towards the top of the drive. 'Wow, it's a bit ancient, though. Looks heavy too. Are you OK with it?'

Summer glanced at his red bike – so much more modern and no doubt much speedier. She shrugged. 'I had a go yesterday.'

She didn't tell him she had been up since seven, riding up and down the lane at the top of the drive so that she wouldn't run the risk of bumping into her uncle or Kenan. They had come back late the evening before. There had been another silent meal with Kenan shooting her 'evils', as Jess would have called them. Then yet another lonely early night.

Don't think about him today.

'So. Where are we going?' she asked.

Zach grinned and pushed off, circled so that he was facing back the way he had come, and called out, 'Follow me!'

Summer quickly got into her stride and bowled along behind Zach. He made a point of checking over his shoulder every so often to make sure she was still with him.

They passed a farm where the air was thick with the sweet, heady smell of hay. Cows were penned in close to the road, lifting their heads to observe soberly as Summer and Zach cycled by.

After a slight dip, the road rose more steeply, and

that was when she saw the stones, standing in a circle, beyond a wooden gate. For a fraction of a second, they looked like people, gathering for a sombre meeting. They were in fact large menhirs, hewn from the same heavy, dark grey granite that Bosleven was made from – and the rocky beach.

Wonder what they're for . . .

Before she could ask Zach, he slowed down and shouted to her to follow, then he veered off the road towards the field where the stones were, as if he had read her curiosity. He dismounted his bike by the gate and leaned it there, waiting for her.

'See those?' he said, gesturing as Summer drew level with him. 'Know what they are?'

She pulled a face and shook her head.

He leaned in closer as if about to impart a mystery. Summer flinched. His attitude put her in mind of Kenan teasing her about ghosts on the side path at the house. But Zach said, 'Standing stones.'

Summer snorted. 'Well, obviously,' she said. 'I can see that.'

'No, that's what they are – what they're called. They were put there by the ancient Celts, thousands of years ago.'

'Right,' Summer said. 'Thanks for the history lesson.'

'D'you want to take a closer look? There's a story behind them,' Zach chattered on, oblivious to her sarcasm.

'They're known around here as the Merry Maidens. It's one of Gran's favourite tales – remember I told you she's always full of stories? Come on.'

He leaped over a stile to the right of the gate, which Summer saw was locked, and sprinted up to the stones.

Summer followed. Zach had reached the middle of the circle and whirled round once, his arms spread wide, his face tipped up to the sky. Summer watched him and was seized by the urge to run full pelt into the middle of the circle and join him there at the centre point. She reached him as he began to spin round and round. One of his hands brushed against hers and he grabbed it and then reached for the other, and then they were both spinning, the world around them whisking itself into a blur as it shot past their eyes.

Merry-go-round. Merry Maidens.

She accelerated, spinning faster and faster, her eyes closed now, giggles bubbling up inside her.

Maybe if I spin long enough I'll slip through time. Be spirited away. Back to before all this . . .

Zach laughed and let go of her, and the two of them juddered and staggered, and then sat down heavily on the dry, spiky grass. Zach shrugged off his rucksack, flopped backwards and lay down, arms and legs spread like a star, and stared at the sky.

'Whoa! Makes your head go wild, doesn't it?' he said.

Summer laughed breathlessly and flopped down next to him, watching the sky spin above her, making her feel as though she were still moving. Large white clouds had gathered since the early morning and were now racing beneath streaks of lighter cloud above; only patches of blue could be seen in between. 'Enough to make a pair of sailor's trousers', as her mother would have said.

Mum. There she goes again, finding a way in.

It wasn't that Summer wanted to forget her. It hurt, though, when memories and feelings came and went like this, as though she had no control over them. They surfaced when she least expected them, when she had thought she was thinking about something completely different. Or about nothing at all.

'So d'you want to hear the story, or what?' Zach was saying.

Summer turned her attention to him. 'OK.'

He began telling her the legend: how a group of girls had been dancing in the field on the Sabbath while two pipers played. 'It was forbidden to dance on a Sunday because it was a holy day, and so the girls were turned to stone as punishment.'

'That's not fair!' Summer exclaimed. 'What about the pipers? They shouldn't have been playing either.'

Zach propped himself up on one elbow and looked down on her, grinning. 'Don't worry. They didn't get away with it. Their stones are in a field up the road. They

166

ran off when they saw the dancers turn to stone, but they didn't get very far.'

Summer was aware of how close he was, could feel the warmth of his breath on her cheek.

Zach's grin had faded and he looked suddenly grave. He held her gaze.

Is he going to kiss me?

Summer stiffened slightly, not knowing what to do next, whether to close her eyes or move towards him. She stayed perfectly still, and waited.

Something in her face must have made Zach change his mind, however, for he backed off and stared ahead at the stones instead.

He cleared his throat. 'Sorry, bit of a rubbish story, I guess.'

Summer felt disappointment wash through her. She blushed at the realization that she had wanted him to make the first move.

Summer sat up. 'No, no, it's not.' She forced a lightness into her voice which she did not feel. 'It's kind of sad, actually. If it's true, that is.'

'Yeah?'

'Think about it: one minute the girls were having a laugh with the pipers, dancing, wheeling around in a circle – a bit like us . . .' She paused. 'The next they were gone, turned to cold, lifeless stone.'

Great, I've gone and made it all heavy now.

Zach nodded. 'You're right. I have thought that too. I find myself thinking sometimes . . . this is going to sound . . . Oh, I don't know!'

'Go on. Tell me.'

Zach hesitated. 'Promise you won't laugh? It's just I wonder if that is what it's like to die? One minute you're warm, living, breathing; the next, cold, lifeless as stone. You know? I mean, what's it like, to go from one state to the next, just as though someone has flicked a switch – or waved a witch's wand?'

As he spoke, Summer felt she had gone as cold as stone herself.

Was that what it had been like for her mum? But no – her mum had not gone straight away; she had hung on, suspended, comatose. It had not been a quick flick of a wand – a blink-of-an-eye change from one state to another. She had slipped away slowly.

'Sorry, I've freaked you out,' said Zach. He touched her arm. 'I shouldn't have said that, not after you told me about your mum.' He spoke in a rush.

Summer shook her head. 'It's OK,' she said. 'It's good to talk to someone who understands. I mean, you lost your dad too.'

Zach shuffled closer and put his arm around her shoulders.

Summer leaned into him.

Maybe I should tell him. Right now. About the phone

call, about seeing Mum at the house . . .

A swallow swooped low and fast, its sickle-shaped wings scything through the air, making a swooshing noise which started Summer out of her reverie. She followed the dance of the swallow until it reached the gate.

There was a figure by the bikes. It was a woman. She was staring at the bike Summer had borrowed. She had put her hand out to it.

She's going to nick it!

Summer was on her feet, knocking Zach off balance in her haste. She waved her arms, yelling, 'Hey! Leave that—!' She took a couple of hurried steps forward, stumbling, then broke off, fixed to the spot.

No. Not again.

Her mother. Just the same as Summer had seen her at Bosleven, in the porch and at the piano.

'Mum!' She was screaming now, tripping over her feet to get to the gate.

In the second that she had faltered, in the second that shock had prevented her from reacting quickly enough, her mother had gone, dipping behind the hedges that lined the road, disappearing from view.

Summer careered down the slope.

You are so stupid. Why are you running? You went to her funeral. She is dead.

She reached the stile, clambered over, scraping her

knees, jumped and looked wildly up and down the road. No one.

She's dead, you stupid, stupid idiot. Dead.

Zach had caught up with her. He had been shouting, but she had not heard. 'Summer? What is it?' He put a hand on her shoulder.

She fell against him, grabbing him to her, letting him put both arms around her. Her sobs were muffled as she clutched at him, wetting his T-shirt with her tears.

She didn't know how long they stood like that, but Zach was the first one to gently prise her away and push her hair from her face.

You've blown it. He's not going to want to know you now.

'I'm sorry,' she said shakily.

'It's all right. I know,' he said. 'When someone dies, I mean. It takes a while to understand they are never coming back.'

Summer took a shuddering breath. Then: 'I – I thought I saw her.'

'Maybe you did.'

She looked up at him sharply.

He wasn't laughing at her, though. He shrugged.

'What do you mean?'

'Gran loves going on about these ancient circles. I've always thought it was a load of rubbish, but . . . well, maybe it isn't all nonsense.'

Summer told herself that he was only trying to comfort her. 'Yeah? So what does she say about them?'

'Gran says there are places in Cornwall where time shifts.' Zach spread his hands and gave an embarrassed chuckle. 'Well, it's true that it's an ancient land, Cornwall – and a land that was full of mysticism. Wow, listen to me, going on like an old hippy!'

'No, tell me. I want to know. No one's told me anything about this place,' Summer insisted.

'OK,' Zach said carefully. 'Thing is, loads of people – visitors, tourists and that – come here because they believe there's still something spiritual about the place. If you know what I mean. Gran's got plenty of old stories; says there are "thin places", where she can feel the old land calling to her.'

Summer felt a chill again. It crept along her neck. 'W-what does *that* mean?'

'I don't know. She's a mad old bat sometimes!'

Summer was not going to let him laugh it off. 'Come on, explain,' she insisted.

Zach shrugged. 'You could ask her yourself. Bet you're hungry . . .' He shot her a cheeky grin. 'Gran loves nothing better than to feed people. So?'

'Yeah, that'd be good,' she said quietly.

They walked back to the bikes. Summer rested her head into the crook of Zach's arm, draped around her shoulders. A small glow of happiness nestled inside her.

Chapter Eighteen

Summer and Zach were cycling along the lanes again. The hedges eventually fell away and in their place were houses on one side and a school on the other. The tower of St Gerran church rose ahead of them, gunmetal-grey against the cloud-studded sky: the tallest building by far, surrounded by tiny cottages. Zach took them round the back of the church, down a lane and up to the door of a particularly small terraced cottage with pink walls, a climbing rose hanging over the front door and net curtains at the windows.

Picture-postcard.

He opened the front door and called through. 'It's only me – brought a friend back!' He turned to Summer and gestured to show she should follow.

A faint voice called back, something indistinct, but the tone was friendly.

'What should I do with the bike?' Summer asked, glancing at the dirty tyres.

'Bring it in. It's OK,' he said. 'Prop it next to mine, against the radiator.'

She did as he suggested, then followed him down the narrow hall to a room at the back. Zach's rangy figure blocked the small doorway, so that she had to wait until he had gone into the room before she could make out any details. He was already jabbering away to his gran as Summer entered behind him.

The room was compact and full of furniture and knick-knacks, but impeccably tidy nonetheless. Zach's gran was sitting by a large window which flooded the room with sunlight. She had been knitting. The needles and wool were now resting in her lap as she smiled up at her grandson with the same twinkling blue eyes as his. She flicked a glance in Summer's direction and her face crinkled into a wider smile.

'So. Summer, this is Gran – Molly Pendred. Gran, this is Summer – the girl I told you about, down on the beach,' said Zach. 'She's staying at the Trewarthas'.'

'Oh yes, the girl on the beach,' the old lady said teasingly. 'You're up at Bosleven, are you? Well . . .' She peered more closely at Summer. Then, frowning, she said, so quietly that Summer wasn't sure she had heard properly: 'My, you are the spit—'

'Er, Gran, before you start with your inquisition . . .' Zach fidgeted, embarrassed. 'We're kind of thirsty. Can we grab a drink? Hot work, cycling. Yeah?' He threw the question at Summer.

'Yeah.'

Zach's gran set her knitting to one side and made to get out of her chair. 'Let me get some cake. You youngsters are always hungry!'

'No, it's OK.' Zach put a hand out. 'We'll get it. D'you want anything? Cup of tea?'

'Yes, Zachary dear, that would be lovely.' She was still inspecting Summer very carefully.

Zach shepherded Summer out of the room and led her into a tiny galley kitchen on the left.

'What did she mean, just then?' Summer asked in a low voice.

'Nothing.' Zach was flustered now, fiddling noisily with the tea things and opening and shutting cake tins. 'I mean . . . I'm sorry about Gran. She's great. Really. You'll love her. It's just . . . she can be a bit nosy,' he gabbled, 'and sometimes she just comes out with things – you know how old people can be. Don't take any notice. She'll probably ask you loads of questions – only cos we don't often have visitors, you know? I mean, people come round, like neighbours and that. But we know everyone round here already. Nothing new to say to them any more: a stranger's a bit of excitement for her, so it's only natural she wants to find out all about you! Ah, here we go. Cake.' He lifted it out of a blue-flowered tin and put it on a plate.

Summer felt uneasy at the idea of Mrs Pendred wanting to 'find out all about' her. Still, being here was better than being stuck at Bosleven, skulking around, avoiding Kenan. She thought of how it would be if she had to introduce Zach to her relatives. She could not imagine Zach, with his easy-going manner, hitting it off with the hostile Kenan or awkward Tristan.

'So have you got any mates in the village?' Summer asked.

Zach looked up from loading a tray with the tea things and the cake, which was a garish golden-yellow and studded with sultanas. 'Saffron cake,' he said, seeing her looking at it. 'Delicious!' Then: 'Yeah, I've got mates. But not friends.' He paused. 'Sounds a bit . . . rubbish. What I mean is, I've got people I've hung around with since forever, but – they don't want to do the kind of things I'm into.'

'Like fishing and swimming?'

'Yeah, like that.' Zach grinned. Her stomach flipped. 'They only want one thing now,' he went on. 'To go into town. You know, go to the arcades, hang out. With girls, mostly.' He busied himself with the plates and mugs again.

Summer smiled to herself.

They went back into the sitting room. Zach's gran had stowed her knitting in a basket at her feet and cleared a low table for the drinks and cake. She showed them a chair each and Zach poured the tea.

'So, Summer, where did you spring from?'

Summer started at the old lady's direct manner.

Zach plunged in. 'Summer's mum died.' He shot Summer an apologetic glance.

Wow, OK. No small talk, then!

Zach's gran also looked taken aback at her grandson's opening line. She frowned at him.

'No, it's OK, Mrs Pendred,' Summer said. 'Mum died, yes, and, well, I didn't know it, but it turns out I have family down here, so I came down to Bosleven to be with them. Tristan Trewartha's my uncle. And my guardian.'

Mrs Pendred raised her eyebrows, her mouth a small, surprised 'O'.

'It's . . . a bit weird,' Summer blurted out. 'I'd never met him before, see, and then after Mum died, I found out in her will that Tristan was my guardian. Mum hadn't told anyone about it. Definitely hadn't told me. I didn't even know I had an uncle – and I didn't know Mum had sorted out a guardian for me in case – well . . .' She let out a shaky sigh. 'I – I'm finding it all really strange being here at all, to be honest,' she said.

Mrs Pendred leaned forward and lightly touched her knee. Summer looked at the bird-like hand, its thin fingers knotted with blue veins and the mottled marks of age. Her eyes clouded as she saw her mum's hands on the hospital sheets – thin too, but smooth and white. They would never grow gnarled like this old lady's.

'Summer, d'you mind if I tell Gran what happened

176

just now?' Zach asked, his gentle voice breaking into Summer's thoughts. 'She can tell you more about the things I was talking about. Maybe . . . ?'

Summer chewed her bottom lip. Didn't dare look him in the eye. 'I . . . I don't know,' she muttered. 'I feel stupid now.'

'What have you been up to, Zachary?' His gran pretended to reprimand him.

Zach laughed. 'Nothing! I took Summer to the Merry Maidens. She didn't know about them. She wanted to know the story, and then after I told her, well . . .' He looked at Summer. She gave a small shake of her head. 'Listen, don't be scared,' he said to her. 'Gran won't laugh.'

He is taking me seriously, isn't he?

Summer looked at him. 'You say,' she said in a whisper.

So Zach launched into a description of what had occurred earlier at the stone circle. Summer was grateful that he left out the bit about them whirling round together. He went into detail about the conversation they had had, about how he had heard Summer cry out.

'I saw the woman too, Gran. I know Summer wasn't faking it. She really thinks it was her mum. And, I hope you don't mind me saying this –' he glanced in Summer's direction – 'but it really upset her. It wasn't like she had just seen someone who *looked* like her mum. It was like

177

she'd seen – well, a ghost . . . I told her about the thin places. I thought maybe you would be able to explain?' he finished.

The old lady's smile had faded while her grandson was talking. When he finished speaking, there was a long silence which stretched out into the corners of the tiny room.

Will she say there's a perfectly reasonable explanation? Will she laugh at me?

When Mrs Pendred finally spoke, she was anything but dismissive. 'So,' she said. 'You want to know about thin places?'

Summer nodded.

'Do you know what I mean about there being places where you sense the past is there, alongside the present, maybe even watching you?'

'I . . . I'm not sure.'

'Not everyone is paying enough attention to notice, of course,' Zach's grandmother went on. 'Especially these days. Too many distractions in the modern world. But some people feel it more deeply than others. Some people are more alive to the energy.' Her cool blue eyes locked with Summer's, then she said, 'I think you do know what I am talking about.'

Tristan had talked about energy too.

Zach said jokily, 'Don't go freaking her out, Gran!'

Summer's throat had gone very dry. She shakily

picked up her mug of tea and sipped at it. She thought of the unsettling things that had happened to her back at the house – the noises she had heard, the moving books, that laughter behind the bookcase – and of how she had definitely seen her mother more than once now. Then there was that phone call the night her mother had died . . .

'Are you all right?' Zach had his hand on her arm. 'You look a bit . . . pale.' He was evidently regretting putting her in this situation. 'Gran, I think maybe we should leave it.'

Summer set her mug down gently on the low table. 'I . . . there's been other things,' she began, ignoring Zach. Her voice was unsteady. 'It's not just what happened today. Not only since I've been here either.' She stopped and looked up at Mrs Pendred. 'I don't know if I can talk about it. You'll think I'm being weird. You don't know me.'

Zach's grandmother gave a small smile and shook her head. 'If Zachary likes you, that's all I need to know.' She said it with such certainty, such kindness. Summer knew then that she was safe. It would be OK. She looked at Zach. He smiled too, encouraging her.

So she told them everything, starting with the phone call. The only thing she didn't tell them about was finding those photos. Guilt prevented her.

Zach and his gran listened intently, occasionally

sipping at their tea and nibbling their slices of cake, but otherwise making no interruption. Finally, Summer stopped talking and sat back in her chair, relief flooding through her: at last she had been able to unburden herself.

The old lady's milky-blue eyes were tender. 'You're not being silly, you know. Just grieving,' she said.

Summer saw that Zach's face was full of sadness.

What was it he said? 'When someone dies . . . It takes a while to understand they are never coming back.'

A swell of heartache rose up in Summer.

They don't believe I saw or heard anything at all.

She blinked hard and stared at her hands, digging her fingernails into her palms.

'Just grieving.' My mind playing tricks on me.

Zach prised her hands apart, took one in his and gave it a light squeeze. Summer didn't dare look up, but she allowed herself a squeeze back while Mrs Pendred continued. 'Grief can open doors that would normally be firmly held closed. We know something of this energy – don't we, Zachary dear?'

Zach merely gave a 'Hmm' in reply.

His gran sighed. 'There are all sorts of emotions we have that are . . . day-to-day, you could say. They can be strong too, of course: anger, jealousy, that kind of thing. But you should not underestimate the power of grief: we only grieve because we love, and love is the most powerful emotion of all.'

Summer glanced up. Those light blue eyes, so twinkly a minute ago, were dull. As though a veil had been drawn across them.

'In a perfect world,' Mrs Pendred went on, more softly, 'at your age, you should not have had to discover the painful side of loving someone. I am so sorry for you. Losing your mum – that's a terrible thing.'

Summer swallowed. 'Thanks,' she whispered. 'It's . . . it's good to talk to someone who understands.'

'Oh, I understand, all right. A loss like that shakes a person, makes them feel and notice things they'd never notice otherwise,' the old lady said. 'You need to know that ghosts are not necessarily bad, though. They don't have to be frightening things.'

Summer frowned. 'Why do you say that?'

'Gran . . .' Zach's voice sounded a warning.

'It's OK,' said Summer. 'I want to know. If your gran knows about these things, I need her to tell me. Please?'

'If there has been a lot of love in life, it stands to reason that some of it must remain after death,' said Mrs Pendred. 'Your mother loved you dearly, Summer, and wanted you to go to a place that meant a lot to her, where she knew you would be safe. Maybe she is trying to tell you this now, because she could not tell you while she was still with you. Not all spirits are bad, dear,' she finished.

181

Tristan had said something like that – about his wife's parents. That they were still part of Bosleven. And Mum must have been. Those photos proved it, didn't they?

Summer's eyes pricked with tears. She battled to keep control of her voice. 'So you think Mum had a special reason for sending me to live at Bosleven.'

It was no good, she could not stop herself; the tears had begun to roll slowly down her cheeks. Zach rubbed his thumb on her hand comfortingly, which made her cry all the more.

'Don't resist that door, dear,' said Mrs Pendred, leaning forward to pat her arm. 'Don't try and keep it closed if it wants to be opened. Keeping things held in is never good for us. Don't be frightened to think of your mum and let her speak to you. That's the only way you'll find out what it is she wants you to know.'

Chapter Nineteen

Summer met Zach every day for the next week. This was what she had been missing, ever since coming to Bosleven: having something to look forward to. Hot summer days with someone who only had to smile at her to warm her from the inside out; endless hours in the fresh air, away from the house – and away from Kenan, and everything that was bothering her.

Her thoughts of home, of Jess, were only fleeting now. When she did think of her friend, it was as though she were remembering a character in a book or a film. Jess had become unreal to her.

Summer and Zach had quickly fallen into a routine: meeting down on the rocks early in the day; swimming immediately if the tide was right; if not, a spot of fishing first. Climbing too; exploring every rock, every boulder. Sheltering in the caves as a freak shower passed over. Sharing picnics they had brought down to the beach with them. Lighting fires with driftwood as the sun sank over the bay. Then back to his house for tea and a natter with Zach's gran.

He took her to Lamorna. It was another wide arc of rocky beach, around the headland from 'their' beach, as she had come to think of it. It was beautiful too, but tourists came to rent boats and to buy drinks and ice creams in the cafe on the pier. It was not the wild, secret place that their beach was.

Summer wondered if it had been, once. When her mother was a girl.

She had told Zach about her middle name.

'It is a pretty popular name around here,' he said. 'When Gran was a girl, she knew a couple of Lamornas. There's a girl in my class too.'

Maybe Mum called me that as a way of remembering this place.

The thought pleased her. It was another link in the chain of clues that made her feel she belonged here.

Summer was happier, healthier and stronger than she could ever remember feeling. Her pasty white skin had developed a glow, and her dark hair was shot through with streaks of sun-bleached caramel. She had never thought of herself as an outdoor kind of girl. Now she wanted nothing more than to be out, down on the rocks, cycling through the lanes. She did ask herself if she would feel the same about the place if Zach were not there with her, but knew what the answer was. She was excited about meeting him every day; no doubt about that.

Tristan never asked where she was going beyond a

simple 'Out again?' He seemed relieved that Summer did not ask anything of him beyond a sandwich and a bottle of water. In return he asked nothing of her.

Her uncle had warmed to her, it seemed. At mealtimes he made the effort to exchange the odd word or two, but Kenan's silences (when he bothered to turn up at all) had lengthened and deepened and were punctuated with nasty sneers at Summer when he thought Tristan wasn't looking.

Tristan had only once asked what she did with her time.

'Oh, you know. Just out and about. Exploring. Reading.' It was only half a lie.

It was enough to put him off the scent. 'That's great. Make the most of this lovely weather. As long as you're OK being on your own so much?'

Kenan had glared harder than ever after that. 'Yeah, as long as you're *OK*, Summer,' he had hissed.

Summer's new-found happiness meant she was gradually relenting in her feelings towards her cousin. He was hurting as much as she was, she reasoned, as there was still no sign of his mother returning. She decided to make a renewed effort not to react to Kenan's hostility.

Tristan caught her one morning as she was about to slip out and meet Zach.

'Glad I caught you before you disappeared!' he

exclaimed. 'I'm sorry I've been a bit . . . preoccupied lately. I'll take you into Penzance if you like?' He ruffled his hair and made an attempt at a smile.

The lines around his eyes and mouth were deeper than ever, his eyes circled, dark. Summer felt a stab of guilt as it dawned on her that she had not taken much notice of him lately.

Looks like he hasn't slept in weeks.

'So? Do you want to go now? It's about time I got you that phone. Perhaps we should think about what you need for school too. You'll be starting in a month.'

'S-sorry?' Summer was shocked. Hadn't he said that they would be visiting schools, that she would have some say in where she went? It was something that had seemed years in the future, something she had no need to think about yet. She wanted to concentrate on nothing beyond the here and now.

Tristan was immediately apologetic. 'Sorry, I didn't mean to spring that on you. We'll have to talk about it, though. Term will be here before we know it! Maybe we'll leave it for today . . . Just shopping for now, then. That is, unless you have plans?' His brow wrinkled.

'No, no.' Summer could see how much it had cost him to make the first move.

How do I get out of this?

A couple of weeks ago she would have jumped at

Tristan taking any sort of interest in her. But not today.

Zach will be waiting. Wonder where he goes to school . . .

'You might like to have a look at the shops on Causewayhead,' her uncle suggested. 'Mosey around while I do a couple of jobs. Can't have you trailing around the shops with an old man like me, eh?'

She raised her eyebrows at that.

He gave a short laugh. 'OK, so you have a wander, then when I'm done, we'll see if you need anything. Maybe go to look at phones?'

Summer nodded dumbly. She did not care about getting a new phone any more. Who would she call? She was more concerned with how she might get out of this little expedition.

'Is Kenan coming?' she asked, keeping her voice light.

Please say no.

'Er – no . . .'

Phew.

'I thought I'd let him lie in. He was with friends last night. I went and fetched him quite late. He's not much of a one for shopping anyway!' he quipped.

Makes two of us.

Jess had been the shopper. Summer had never seen the point. Not having much in the way of pocket money, she had never been able to buy anything, so she had just trailed around with Jess, enjoying her company but quickly feeling fed up and restless with tramping the pavements.

She reluctantly followed Tristan out to the car. She saw him glance fleetingly back at the house, as though checking for something. Did her uncle feel the same watchful presence she felt in those walls?

'Here.' Tristan interrupted her thoughts, taking her by surprise and pressing something into her hand.

Summer instinctively pulled back, but her uncle closed her fingers firmly over the object which dug into her flesh.

Fixing her with his dark eyes Tristan said kindly, 'Take it. Can't have you roaming the streets with no spending money, can we?' and smiled.

Summer looked down at her hand. Nestling in her palm was a crumpled note. He had given her twenty quid.

'Thanks,' she murmured.

It was generous of him, but Summer was embarrassed, particularly as she would rather not be going into Penzance at all.

As the car bumped along the drive she stared out of the window and wondered anxiously what Zach would think when she failed to meet him on the rocks.

Tristan pointed out various shops to her before disappearing to do his errands.

'You must tell me if there is anything you need,' he told her. 'I – I know I should have asked you this when you first arrived. I thought maybe Becca would . . . Anyway, please ask. Don't be shy.'

'It's fine, really.' Summer knew she should be grateful for his kindness, but it was all a bit too much, this sudden attention. It had been much easier when he ignored her and left her to her own devices. She was relieved when he went, even though the cobbled street he left her on was lined with ridiculously touristy shops which held nothing of interest for her.

Who on earth would want to buy a pirate's fancy dress costume?

She bought herself a lurid blue Slush Puppie from a kiosk outside the cinema and sipped at it tentatively, her teeth fizzing with the shocking sweetness and cutting cold. Then she sat on a bench and stared ahead at a large, rambling bargain basement shop that seemed to sell everything from art materials to hardware, and wondered how she would pass the hour until she had to meet Tristan again.

Her uncle met her in the car park at the top of the cobbled street. He was leaning against the car, flicking through a newspaper and didn't look up until she said hello.

'Oh!' he jumped, as though he had not expected her; had forgotten about her, maybe. Then he smiled. 'Let's go then. Hope you don't mind, but I passed the phone shop so I thought I might as well get you a mobile.' He reached down and handed her a bag.

So. No say in which school I go to. No say in which phone I get.

'Right. Thanks.'

'You still won't get any reception at the house, I'm afraid, but at least you've got one for when you're out and about. I should have thought of that earlier. You might need to contact me. If anything happened or . . .'

'Thanks,' Summer repeated, turning the box over in her hands. She knew she should sound more pleased, but she could not help feeling angry that Tristan had not thought she might want to choose the phone with him.

Wish I could call Zach.

The thought of him, fishing off the rocks, possibly – hopefully – wondering where she was, made her desperate to get back. She swept her self-pitying thoughts aside.

'Are we going now?' she asked.

Tristan looked deflated. 'Yes. Of course.'

I've done it again. Been a cow. He thought he was doing the right thing, bringing me here, buying me a phone.

It was as though she and her uncle spoke completely different languages.

Her uncle drove in silence around the endless mini roundabouts back down to the sea front. There was a crowd of people pouring off a large ferry. It looked like the one she often watched these days from the rocks.

'The ferry is the *Scillonian*,' Tristan spoke at last, seeing her staring at the crowd. 'Takes people to the Scillies. Beautiful islands – golden beaches. Perfect place for a holiday. I should . . .' He stalled, then coughed and went on. 'I should take you there one day?' It was more of a question than a suggestion. When she did not answer, he blurted out, 'I hope you are settling in. I want you to feel at home here, Summer. At Bosleven. It has not been the best start, but I promise things will get easier. Cat – your mum – she wanted you to feel you belonged with us. I know that.' He kept his eyes fixed resolutely on the road ahead.

Summer glanced across at him sharply. It was the first time he had brought up the subject of her mother without being prompted. She knew she should not let the moment pass.

Quick! Think of something to say!

The photos. The ones she had found in the attic, of her mother on the beach. She should ask him now, while he was driving and could not walk away.

The words of Zach's gran came back to her, suddenly, almost as though she were in the car right then. '*Don't try and keep the door closed if it wants to be opened.*

Keeping things held in is never good for us.'

Summer felt queasy as it occurred to her that that was exactly what she had been trying to do – keep the door closed, keep Mum out of this new happiness she had found in her friendship with Zach. She had purposefully stayed away from the house and had given up on looking for more clues since spending time with him.

She swallowed, screwed up her courage, took the plunge.

'Tristan . . . ?'

'Hmm?'

'I . . . I hope you don't mind, but I was kind of exploring around the house the other day. When you were – well, you were busy.'

'Oh yes?'

'Yeah, I . . . I went up to the attic.'

Tristan looked across at her. 'The attic?'

The look on her uncle's face alarmed her. 'It was raining,' she said quickly. 'I – I didn't have anything to do.'

'Right,' he said. A thin smile flickered on his lips. 'Bit of a mess up there!' His voice was strained, she thought.

'Yeah! Loads of cool stuff, though.'

Come on, you've got to ask him.

'Oh, it's all rubbish, really,' he said, concentrating on the road again. 'Old things. Things that – ah – I've forgotten about, mostly.'

'I guess. There were some books I – I looked at them. And . . .'

Go on!

She was staring ahead too now, not daring to look at him.

I can't do this. I can't tell him . . .

'Some photos. I am sure they were of Mum—'

'Oh, *hell*!' Tristan thumped the steering wheel, hitting the horn by mistake. It blared, sending a shard of fear through Summer, bringing back a sudden, unwanted memory.

Mum, lying in the road.

The driver's horn had blasted out then. The same piercing klaxon. An alarm call.

Tristan was peering at the dashboard and biting his lower lip. He turned to look at Summer, who had gone white.

'I'm so sorry, Summer. I didn't mean to frighten you.' He pointed at a dial in front of him. 'The car's overheating,' he said. 'Such a pain. I'm going to have to pull over and check the radiator.'

Fright turned quickly to annoyance. He had scared the life out of her, slamming down on the horn, shouting like that. Was this an elaborate trick to shut her up? He had done it the minute she had mentioned the pictures.

Overheating? Yeah, right. Just didn't want to hear what I was going to say about the attic, more like.

193

He must know about those photos.

Her heart was still fluttering, even as she muttered inwardly at her uncle.

He had stopped and popped the bonnet. Opening his door he said, 'You'd better get out too. Safer.' His voice had an edge to it; Summer did as she was told.

They walked around to the front of the car, Tristan frowning all the while.

'Well, it doesn't *look* hot, at least,' he said, gesturing to the bonnet. 'No steam. Can't be too hot then. Not yet anyway.'

Spare me the performance.

Tristan pulled his sleeve down over his hand and lifted the bonnet, exposing the maze of pipes and box-like structures that comprised the engine. He did seem genuinely preoccupied.

Either he's a good actor, or . . .

'Aha!' Tristan exclaimed, as though finding the answer to a crossword clue. Then he reached forward, his sleeve still protecting his hand and tentatively touched a blue plastic lid, rather like the lid of a milk bottle. Seemingly reassured, he grasped it and turned it until it came off in his hand.

'Very odd,' he said, half to himself, as he peered in more closely. 'The fluid's at the right level. Not too hot at all in there.' He ruffled his dark hair with his free hand and straightened up, staring at the engine for a moment.

194

Then shaking his head he hastily screwed the cap back on again.

'So it's OK?' Summer asked.

She had lost all confidence in bringing up the subject of the photos now. The moment had passed. Her mouth was sticky from the Slush Puppie, its coldness already long forgotten, and the back of her neck was sweaty from the sun's rays, reflecting off the white houses in the street. She imagined dipping her feet in the Pool, allowing the delicious shock of the water to send shivers up her body. A shock she had feared so recently and now relished.

She thought of Zach again.

He'll have given up by now.

'Come on, let's get you back. You must be hungry,' Tristan was saying.

Summer broke out of her reverie and climbed into the passenger seat once more.

'I think I ought to get the car checked over. Something's not right,' her uncle continued, again as though talking to himself. His eyes flicked repeatedly to the dashboard and he gestured with his left hand briefly to the temperature gauge before him. 'The needle was in the red, but it seems OK now. Oh well. I'll drop you back at the house, then I'll run along to the little garage in St Gerran. Better safe than sorry.'

Summer was no longer listening to this stream of chatter. She sat back and shut her eyes, drowsy with heat.

She pushed aside any niggling fears of her uncle hiding things from her and concentrated instead on the thought that she would get away to the beach as soon as they got back to Bosleven.

Hoping that Zach would have waited after all.

Chapter Twenty

Zach was there, fishing as usual. Summer joined him and after a few minutes of casting and reeling in the line without catching anything, she brought up the subject that was burning her up inside.

'I've been thinking about what your gran said – about letting my mum in?' she said. 'D'you know what she meant?'

'Probably nothing!' Zach said carelessly. 'I wouldn't worry about it.'

'No,' Summer insisted. 'She meant something by it. You know she did.' Summer was not going to let him brush her aside. She had not talked to him about this for days. She needed him to listen, to take her seriously.

Zach read her emotions in her face. 'I think . . .' he said carefully. 'I think she was talking about how it's OK to give in to everything to do with your mum – her death, what she means to you, how you remember her. That kind of stuff. Maybe you should try talking to your uncle more. Tell him how you feel. Gran told me once that people who keep that kind of thing bottled in, well, they can get – ill with it . . .' he tailed off.

Summer pressed him to continue. 'So did she – talk to you like that when your dad died?'

'Hmm.' Zach nodded. He opened his mouth then swallowed, as though changing his mind about saying something. 'I . . . I didn't want to talk about it at all, you see. It was easier to keep it wrapped up inside. It hurt too much to even think about him.' There was a sharp note of bitterness in his voice; his expression was strained.

Summer touched him lightly on the arm.

Zach relaxed a little, taking her hand in his. 'There was Gran, wanting to talk about all of it. All the time. I mean, he was her son and everything, so I guess that's normal. I don't know . . . I think sometimes people like to talk about things to sort them out, and sometimes people like to keep things to themselves. I'm one of those who like to keep things locked away from other people.' He looked down. 'From most other people, that is.'

'I'm sorry,' said Summer. She squeezed his hand. 'You don't have to tell me everything. I only wanted to ask you what your gran had meant about me.'

'It's OK,' Zach said, warmth creeping back into his voice. 'I think meeting you is kind of . . . Maybe we were meant to meet.' He paused. 'Gran says things are either meant to be or not meant to be. I think . . .' He stopped.

'What?' Summer persisted.

'Nothing,' said Zach quickly. He gazed out to sea, then

made a clumsy attempt to change the subject. 'See how calm it is today?'

'Yeah.' She didn't mind. She had not enjoyed seeing him upset. She wanted him back to the way he always was: light and carefree, sunny and bright.

'Know what I'm thinking?'

'No.'

'Let's swim to the Point and climb back.' He turned and grinned at her, his face alight with its usual enthusiasm and excitement. 'Come on!' he said, noting her hesitation. 'I said I'd take you one day – no time like the present. Don't often get totally calm days like this.'

'I . . . I'm not that good a swimmer.'

'Sure you are! I've seen you,' Zach said.

'You've only seen me mucking about in the Pool.'

'Listen, I told you, didn't I? The salt helps to keep you afloat – it's not like doing lengths in an indoor swimming pool. You don't get tired so quickly, honest. There's no swell today – see how flat it is. Anyway, if you stick with me you'll be fine. Promise.'

Summer looked doubtful. 'Really?'

Zach pulled a face. 'Don't you trust me?' he teased. 'I know this bay inside out. If you do get tired, we can always swim back in and get out on the rocks. No problem.' He was already up and tugging at his T-shirt, pulling it over his brown shoulders. His shorts doubled as trunks, so he was ready in a flash.

Summer had her swimmers on under her jeans and top. The thought of swimming so far bothered her. She was not going to admit that to Zach, though.

'OK. Ready,' she said, wriggling out of her clothes and scraping her hair back.

Zach beamed. 'Water's high so we can dive. Come on!' he urged. His strong limbs glowing, tensed and ready, he leaped to the edge and took up his position to plunge in.

'You first,' said Summer, rubbing her arms in anticipation.

He gave her a knowing wink and then arced through the air and broke the surface with barely a splash.

Such a show-off.

She smiled and waited as she always did until Zach had reappeared, laughing, whooping and horsing around, and then she dived towards him. Not as gracefully as he had, of course, but still . . . It was better than hanging around, dipping a toe in, dithering on the side.

She came up gasping at the shock of it, the joy and exhilaration of it, and took off like a rocket across the bay, shrieking with each stroke, until warmth began creeping back into her bones.

Zach caught up with her. 'Hey! Slow down! So much for not being that great a swimmer. You're beating me today.'

'N-not for l-long,' she stammered, spitting out briny mouthfuls. 'You said it w-would be calm!' she added, wide-eyed at the choppy surface of the water.

'Well, it's always a little rougher out here than it is in the Pool,' he said. 'Sorry. Believe me, though, if you focus on your stroke and keep it steady, you'll be there in no time.'

They swam side by side, Zach on the outside, shielding her from the open waters, the sweep of the rocky cove on the other. Summer did feel safe, knowing she could swim inland if she wanted to, although they were still some way from the shore.

Zach kept talking as he swam, telling her about other expeditions he had made across the bay.

'Do you ever get jellyfish here?' she asked suddenly.

Zach laughed. 'Course we do!'

'Stinging ones?'

'What other kind is there?'

'Thanks a bunch!' she exclaimed.

'No, it's OK. We usually only get them when there's been a storm. You'll be all right.'

The Point did not seem to be getting any closer. Summer's legs were beginning to feel heavy and her fingers seemed to have stiffened; she could no longer hold them together to make effective paddles for her breaststroke.

Zach saw that she was flagging. 'Nearly there,' he said. 'It'll suddenly seem nearer, promise. Do you want a hand?'

'No.'

I have to do this.

He was right, another couple of strokes and the shoreline was within their grasp. She began to count to keep herself focused.

'Thirty, thirty-one, thirty-two . . .'

Zach put on a spurt and suddenly he was holding on to a rock and shouting, 'That's it! Come towards me. This is the best way to get out.'

He waited until she was within spitting distance and then hauled himself out of the water, reaching over to give her a hand. She took it gratefully, certain she did not have the strength to pull herself up. He leaned back and balanced himself on a rock with one hand and then heaved her out with one strong tug of his free hand.

She had turned to jelly. She was numb, her legs useless as she stood shivering on the rock. The sun had dipped down behind the Point and already the heat was going out of the air.

'Best thing is to keep moving,' Zach told her. 'Let's climb the Point. That'll warm us up. Good view from there too. I'll show you where I fish from.'

She raised her head to follow the line of the craggy outcrop and shivered violently, her teeth knocking against each other. The last thing she felt like doing was clambering up that high.

A mug of hot chocolate would be better.

'W-wouldn't we need ropes – climbing equipment?'

Zach took one of her hands again and rubbed it between his. 'No. It's easy! Come on, you'll be fine in a minute or two.'

He was right. After the first few shaky steps she found she was concentrating so hard on following him as he jumped, sure-footed and nimble, she had stopped thinking about the cold. By the time they reached the last, tricky, scrambly bit of the climb, she was almost too warm from the exertion.

Zach navigated the steep section to the top of the Point like a practised mountaineer, his feet finding little notches and footholds that Summer would not even have noticed on her own. She followed him, her toes gripping into the crevices, her fingers pulling herself up. Zach reached the top and leaned over to help her up beside him.

'Ta-daaa!' he cried, dramatically sweeping his arm out in a victorious salute. 'Look at that.'

Summer followed his gaze. Three small sailing boats skimmed along the inky line of the horizon, their sails paper cut-outs against the purple-blue cloudless sky. A shag, its wings petrol-black, its neck snake-sleek and graceful, made a sudden, clean dive into the water as Zach had done earlier, and re-emerged moments later with a fish in its beak.

'Isn't this just the most beautiful place you've ever seen?' Zach said.

His face was almost sad, it was so wistful; as if he wished he could capture the Point, the sea, and hold on to it just as it was. Fold it away and keep it, just for him.

Or maybe that's what I want.

'It is,' Summer said. 'Beautiful.'

She looked down to where they had begun their climb and tipped back on her heels, feeling dizzy as she saw how high they had come.

Zach put a steadying hand on her shoulder. 'Careful!'

She stood firm, but kept her eyes on the rocks beneath. She remembered how she had been when she had first found the beach, after that fight with Kenan.

I wanted everything to end then.

She thought of keeling forward, toppling, falling . . . Would you crash and bounce on to the rocks on the way down, or fall outwards in an arc like the bait on the end of a fishing line? Would you hit the water with a slap, or slice sharply through it? Or would you keep on falling, through the light surface water and then sink down, down like a stone into the suffocating black depths? Perhaps your lungs would fill slowly, painfully. Or maybe you would pass out immediately and then slip gracefully away into oblivion.

Summer looked at Zach, watching her closely, and knew that she no longer wanted to let go of life altogether. She had let go of her old life, that much was true. But in that moment she knew she wanted to grab hold of the future and live it to the full.

I just want to know about you, Mum. About you and Bosleven. Tell me! Please! Then I can move on.

'What are you thinking?' Zach asked.

Summer squirmed.

'Tell me,' Zach insisted.

Summer gave a short, apologetic laugh. 'I was thinking about Mum again. I found these photos. Of her, on the rocky beach. I need to know, Zach. Why won't anyone tell me about her being here? Why didn't she tell me?'

Zach shrugged. 'You've got to ask your uncle. He's the only one who can tell you, I guess.'

'I know.'

I can't keep going on about this to Zach. It's up to me. I'm the only one who can find out the truth.

She blurted out, 'Have you ever thought about jumping off here?'

'What?' Zach cried.

'No, no, I don't mean I want to,' she said quickly. 'I mean . . . maybe I did before.'

'Before what?' Zach said.

She held his gaze. With the sun behind his head, his eyes were dark. She felt goosebumps rise along her arms.

'You know,' she said, turning away.

He caught her elbow and made her look back at him. 'Yeah,' he said.

They stood there, not speaking.

'Come here,' Zach pulled her towards him and kissed her once, lightly, on the lips. Then he held her close and, mumbling into her salty hair, he said, 'I won't let you fall. I promise.'

'I know.' She leaned into him.

He tilted her face towards his. 'Talk to Tristan,' Zach said. 'You can do it.' He kissed her again, longer this time.

She let him wrap his arms around her, felt his heart beating against her.

'Yes,' she smiled. 'Yes, I can.'

Chapter Twenty-one

Summer walked back up to Bosleven feeling light and strong, ready to find Tristan and have it out with him once and for all.

Warm, tempting aromas were coming from the kitchen, awakening a ravenous hunger in Summer. It was the first time she had felt properly hungry for weeks.

She hurried into the kitchen, determined to have the truth from Tristan before she could weaken and let him change the subject.

'Hi,' she said, walking in. 'Oh . . .' Her heart plummeted as she saw Kenan, his arms folded, leaning with his back against the worktop.

He shot her a sneery smile. 'You look a bit *hot and bothered*,' he said and raised one eyebrow in a knowing gesture.

Something about the way he looked at her unnerved her. Did he know about Zach? Had he been watching them?

He's just being a jerk as usual.

She scowled at him and went to get herself a glass of water.

'Ah, Summer. I was just telling Kenan about the car,' Tristan said.

He was at the stove, busying himself with cooking.

'Yeah, yeah. Won't stop going on about it,' Kenan said, pushing himself away from the worktop and throwing himself into a chair at the table where places were laid for supper.

'Well, I'm sorry, Kenan, but it's worrying.' Tristan ladled fish stew into large oval dishes and set them down on the table. 'I've taken the car out a couple more times today and every time the gauge has shot up into the red again.'

Kenan rolled his eyes and began eating, slurping noisily.

Summer ignored him and sat down to her dish of stew, concentrating on inhaling the rich, inviting smell.

Tristan sat next to her. Still he talked, on and on about the car.

'The garage says it's nothing, so I checked the level of fluid in the engine again and it's fine. Nothing's hot when I touch it.'

'Oh for goodness sake!' Kenan exclaimed, banging down his knife and fork. 'Take it BACK to the flipping garage!'

'I have. Twice. I don't get it. Thermostat's fine. It's not even a faulty gauge,' Tristan said.

Summer was not listening properly. She was savouring

the meal and thinking about what Zach had said. '*Talk to Tristan. You can do it.*' She gave a small smile as she remembered his kiss.

'What are you grinning at?' Kenan spat. 'I suppose you think it's funny our car's broken down. Like our family.'

'Kenan!' Tristan looked horrified. 'I have told you already. I will not stand for—'

'For what? What won't you stand for, Dad?' Kenan pushed his food away, the sauce slopping over the edges on to the table. 'For Mum not wanting to set foot in this room with us while *she* is here? Oh no, it's not that that you're upset about, is it? It's a stupid, flipping CAR that has got you upset!'

'Kenan,' Tristan said in a low voice. 'I am warning you . . .'

'What?' Kenan was on his feet now, his chin jutting forward, his stance challenging, furious. 'What are you going to do? Chuck me out? You'd love that, wouldn't you?' he said, turning on Summer.

Tristan pushed back his chair and grabbed his son firmly by the shoulders. 'Calm down,' he insisted. 'I will not have you talk like that to Summer – or to me.'

Kenan was shaking, but he remained silent.

Tristan kept his voice calm. 'How about saying sorry?' he said.

'How about *no*?' Kenan shouted, pushing away from

his father, making for the door. 'If anyone should say sorry, it's HER!'

'Kenan, come back right now,' Tristan said, his voice crackling with emotion.

'No. I'm going to talk to Mum.'

Tristan stiffened.

Kenan shot Summer a look of pure poison and left the room, slamming the door so that it rattled in its frame.

Summer had been paralysed during the scene, but at this she jumped up and went to Tristan's side.

'It's OK,' she said. 'He misses his mum. I get it.'

They both listened as Kenan's heavy footfall echoed in the hall.

Something niggled at Summer.

He said he was going to talk *to her. Is she here, then? In the house? Hiding?*

She dismissed the thought immediately. She would have bumped into her aunt at some point if that were the case.

Must be going to call her, or message her like before or something.

Tristan began gathering up the dishes and cutlery in silence. Summer started to help, not knowing what to say now. Kenan's hateful words hovered in the air between them.

Summer watched as her uncle's brow became furrowed and he worked his mouth as though talking to himself.

210

I'm not going to be able to get anything out of him now. He's too upset.

She decided to turn the conversation back to the car. Even that would be better than this dreadful silence.

'You're really worried. About the engine?' she began quietly.

Tristan looked startled. 'Um . . . oh no. I was just thinking about something else, that's all,' he said. 'Sorry, away with the fairies, as they say.'

Summer checked to see that Kenan was not hovering by the door. She steeled herself, remembering Zach's encouragement.

I have to try and ask him about those photos again. It's stupid, leaving the whole thing buried. There's too much that's not being said in this family. No wonder Kenan's so screwy.

She cleared her throat and said, 'So, erm, I've been meaning to ask you – about the photos?'

'Hmm?'

Something brushed against Summer's leg, distracting her. She glanced down to see the cat, who shot her a peculiar, narrow-eyed look before disappearing into the little sitting room behind the kitchen.

They never cuddle it. Never seen them feed it either, come to that . . .

'Pass me that cloth, can you?' Tristan asked, his tone completely normal again, as though the scene with

Kenan had never happened.

Summer felt irritation prickle along her spine. She was going to get him talking even if it sparked another scene. 'The photos,' she repeated. 'I was asking about them when the car overheated?'

Tristan would not look at her, made a big deal out of scrubbing at a stubborn patch of grease on a pan. 'Oh, were you? I have to say there really is so much junk up in that attic . . .'

They were both speaking at once now.

'They were photos of Mum—'

'I have no idea what half the stuff is—'

'It was her, on the rocky beach—'

'I guess there's probably stuff from ages ago—'

'LISTEN TO ME!' Summer had had enough of him brushing over her, always trying to ignore what she had to say, pushing her aside. 'LISTEN—!'

'CAT!' Tristan was staring at her, his eyes wide, his hand on her shoulder.

'What? Oh, for heaven's sake forget the flipping cat!' Summer shouted.

Looks as though he's seen a ghost!

Tristan gave her a little shake, moving her away from the sink. 'I meant, Summer – stop talking! Sit down – you're bleeding!' Tristan urged.

What?

She put her hand up to her face. It felt wet. She took

212

her fingers away and saw they had dark red smears on them. Tristan caught her by the elbow and pressed a hanky to her face.

'Tilt your head back. It's OK. Just a nosebleed. I used to get them all the time at your age. Has this happened before?'

'Uh-uh.'

'Pinch the bridge of your nose and keep your head tilted. I'll fetch something to cool it.'

'It's OK, there's no need,' Summer said.

Tristan was already scurrying to the freezer, seemingly relieved to have something to do other than answer Summer's questions.

Summer did not get the chance to talk to her uncle alone again that evening. After her nosebleed had stopped, the phone rang. Summer listened in to start with, thinking she might pick up something of interest, but it seemed to be a call regarding a local matter Tristan was involved in. The conversation went on for so long, Summer gave up waiting for him to finish.

She was going to go straight to her room for another early night, but stopped at the top of the first flight of stairs, eyeing the way up to the attic. She had convinced herself by now that Tristan did know about the photos and that he would do anything to avoid talking about them.

Maybe if I fetched some, forced him to look at them.

She was reluctant to go up there alone again, however. She imagined Kenan finding her. Told herself not to be pathetic.

Suddenly the events of the day – the swim, the climb, the nosebleed . . . the very effort of always having to be on her guard in the house, of being a stranger there (whatever Tristan had said) – all this fell on her in a crashing wave of exhaustion.

Just sleep now. Think about it tomorrow.

She turned from the stairs and went into her room.

Summer was sinking, sinking fast. All around her was black. She strained to catch even a sliver of light. There was nothing to guide her, to let her know where she was. She was falling, dropping down through the darkness like a rock from the edge of the cliff.

What will I fall on to? The rocks below? The sea?

But she could not see the rocks or the water. She tried to scream, to attract attention. But whose? There was no one here. Nothing but darkness. She reached out to grasp at something, anything. Her hands closed on thin air. She opened her mouth, uselessly. Straining to make a noise she closed her eyes against the blackness, then . . .

'Huh—?'

She jerked upwards, her heart pulsating, her face wet. She was still surrounded by blackness, but she was awake now and could extinguish the dark with a flick of a switch. The light blazed, momentarily blinding her – but not before she had caught a flash of red on the white sheet. She blinked, rubbed her eyes and forced them to open.

Blood. Lots of it.

Her fingers tentatively touched her nose, her mouth.

Not again!

She scrabbled free of the sheets. Dropping to the floor, she saw that the front of her pyjamas was bloody, and when she took her hand from her face, there was fresh blood on her fingers. She swallowed. A metallic tang filled the back of her throat.

The image of her mother flashed before her again, just as it had when Tristan had hit the car horn.

Lying in the road, blood collecting in a puddle, mixing with her long dark hair – that trickle of black-red from her nostrils . . .

Summer felt the room tilt. She grabbed hold of the side of the bed to steady herself.

OK, calm down. This is not a car crash. Only a nosebleed.

Padding slowly across to the door, she tiptoed out on to the landing. The rest of the house was dark, just as her room had been. No friendly lamp left on for night-time excursions to the loo. She shivered as she felt her way to the bathroom, using the light from her room to guide

215

her; not wanting to announce herself to the rest of the house by turning on any other lights.

Once in the bathroom she turned on the light with one hand; swiftly closed the door behind her with the other. The floor was freezing under her bare feet. Two spots of red fell on to the white tiles.

She looked up and saw herself in the mirror; saw the blood-smeared, white skin, the wide-eyed shock. Repeated to herself to calm down.

It's only a nosebleed, Summer.

So why could she not shake the image of her mother out of her head? She had not thought of this for weeks before today, but now it replayed in her mind over and over on a loop.

The car's brakes screeching.

The sharp scream from her mum.

'Summer, watch out!'

The shock of the crash as the car hit the wall.

The car horn blaring as the driver hit the steering wheel.

And her mother, lying, twisted.

In her own blood.

Summer was shaking as she filled the sink with cold water, splashing some on to her face. Then she pulled off her pyjama top and flung it into the honey-sweet water. Red swirled and mixed, diluting the rust-dark stains.

Her nose was still dripping.

Ice. I'll have to go down to the kitchen.

She tensed at the idea of walking downstairs, alone, in the dark. The quiet was heavy around her, the house closing in on her. The tiniest creak and groan of timbers set her heart skittering.

But I have to do something. I can't go back to bed like this.

Holding her flannel to her face, she went back to the bedroom, grabbed a T-shirt and lowered it gingerly over her head with one hand, keeping a grip on the flannel with the other, the taste of blood, ferric, in the back of her throat.

She fumbled for her torch and found her trainers, cramming her feet into them. Then she crept out and down into the kitchen.

The cat was curled up on the work surface and lifted its head in sleepy greeting. She thought it was safe to turn on a light now. No one would notice, unless they too had woken and come down for a midnight visit.

The animal let out a low *miaow* of protest at being disturbed, but it did not move from its spot. Summer went to the fridge and opened the freezer compartment. She took out a packet of peas and pressed them to her face.

The relief was exquisite, although quickly the cold became a burning sensation. She looked around and saw a tea towel draped over the stove and wrapping the peas in that, held the packet to her nose again.

Sinking into the old armchair by the dresser, she closed her eyes, tilted her head back. The cat jumped lightly on to her lap, and she stroked it absent-mindedly.

She was drifting back to sleep, the bag of frozen peas slipping from her grasp, when the cat suddenly nipped the hand that had been stroking it.

'Hey! What was that for?' she exclaimed.

'*Roooaaaw!*' The cat's pink lips were pulled back over its teeth in a snarl.

It stared at her wildly, its eyes wide, its ears pinned flat. Then it flipped off Summer's lap and bounced on balletic paws to the kitchen door, where it paced up and down, hackles raised, teeth bared.

This strange behaviour sent a shiver down Summer's back.

'What are you doing—?' She stopped with a gasp.

She was sure she had heard footsteps.

Her stomach lurched, even as she told herself not to be stupid.

So what if it's Kenan or Tristan? I'm allowed to sit in the flipping kitchen, aren't I?

She listened. No noise other than from the cat, who was now scratching at the door, seemingly desperate to get out of the room.

Summer slowly got out of the chair and put the peas

on the worktop behind her. Touching her nose gently, she noted with relief that the bleeding had stopped. As she approached the cat, it went into paroxysms; its fur on end, its tail waving a warning. Summer pushed the door open a crack and the cat shot through. She followed it out into the hall where it continued its angry hissing and back-arching, its ears flat as it paced to and fro.

'What are you trying to tell me? There's nothing out here.' Summer turned to go back to the kitchen to put the peas back in the freezer.

Then the ringing began.

The phone in the hall, jarring, high-pitched, pierced the silence like an alarm going off.

Summer was immediately back at Jess's house, answering a phone ringing in the middle of the night; hearing her mother . . . *'Bye, love.'*

No! Not again. Mum?

Summer froze in the doorway.

It wouldn't be Mum. Couldn't be. She's dead! She's DEAD! WHEN ARE YOU GOING TO BELIEVE THAT?

Should she answer the phone? Would it wake the others? Might it be Tristan's wife? Or Kenan – she did not know where he had gone last night.

Then the grandfather clock in the hall began chiming.

What the hell—? The clock never makes a sound. It doesn't work!

The cat yowled and ran away. Summer did not see

where it went; the house was too dark.

The clock struck on and on.

It was sounding the hour – albeit an hour that didn't exist.

Thirteen, fourteen, fifteen. On and on and on . . .

It echoed through the hall, clashing with the shrill phone. Summer whirled from one to the other, decided she could at least do something about the phone, so grabbed the receiver and shouted into it above the noise of the clock, 'Hello? Hello!' The ringing continued as though she had not answered it at all; ringing in her ear and ringing out into the dark house; the striking of the clock and the phone combining in a discordant siren.

Summer dropped the receiver and covered her ears with her hands.

Nightmare! It's a nightmare!

The noise continued. It was real. She wasn't going to wake up out of this.

But if this *was* real, where was Tristan? Surely he would have heard the racket and come running by now?

Then the ringing stopped: both phone and clock were silent.

That is when a low rumbling sound started up. It came from somewhere on the next floor, above the hall.

Summer closed her eyes, willing the house to return to its former stillness, praying in vain that she would wake in her bed in a moment, the sun streaming through the curtains, the rooks and wood pigeons cawing and cooing.

The rumbling overhead increased in urgency.

Then the faint scent of an autumn afternoon filled the air. Smoke. But who would have a bonfire in the middle of the night?

'FIRE!'

Her body sprang back to life.

Where's the cat?

She ran, frenzied, up the stairs, grabbing the wooden banister and swinging herself up, leaping over the steps two at a time. She could not worry about the cat. What about Tristan? Had Kenan come back? Why were they not awake?

This whole place is made of wood. It'll go up like a box of matches.

The fire was coming from the attic: she could see an unearthly orange glow at the top of the stairs. She did not stop to flick on the lights on the half-landing as she hammered on Tristan's door. She heard her own voice screaming as she burst in, not waiting for a response.

'TRISTAN!'

Her uncle's hand reached out from the sheets and fumbled with his bedside light.

'Fire!' Summer pulled back the bedclothes, grabbed her uncle by the shoulders, shaking him, pushing her face into his. 'Got to get Kenan. Get out! QUICK!'

'What?' Tristan fiddled with his pyjama top, running

his hands through his hair, sleep-confused. She left him to follow and ran along the landing to Kenan's room.

There was still no sign of the flames coming closer.

It's all right, we'll get out.

Smoke was seeping down. Summer's eyes watered and she narrowed them against the stinging, choking air. She coughed and dropped instinctively to the floor, obeying some long-distant instruction from a health-and-safety talk at school. Covering her face with one hand, she crawled to her cousin's door, her voice rising in a muffled, hysterical descant over Tristan's.

'Kenan! KENAAAAN!'

A dark shadow appeared above her.

Thank goodness. He's OK.

'Kenan – quickly—!' A hand fell sharply on to her neck. She was dragged backwards, away from the door, back towards Tristan's room.

'It's – all – right—!' She tried to speak, to say she could walk, she was fine.

He thinks I've fallen.

But: 'What have you done? WHAT HAVE YOU DONE?'

Kenan was screaming in her ear, gripping her hair, yanking her head back so that her eyes and throat filled with the smoke that was filling the air now.

What have I done?

'You stupid little cow!' Kenan's voice choked, rasping.

'If you have hurt Mum . . .' He broke out in a fit of coughing, then yelled, 'WHAT THE HELL HAVE YOU DONE?'

Me? Hurt his mum? What—?

His words stunned her like a bolt of lightning. It was as though she were pinned down by the weight of her nightmares again. She felt herself being dragged along the floor, only dimly aware of Tristan screaming something from above her, howling at his son; of Kenan relaxing his hold; of someone lifting her as she heard herself say, 'But it wasn't me . . . wasn't me . . .'

Chapter Twenty-two

Kenan disappeared that night. Tristan told her later, once the fire brigade had put out the fire, the police had come and the paramedics had checked them over. She had been so desperate for him to stop yelling at her, to stop his unbearable accusations, that it had not occurred to her to look out for him while the house was teeming with people.

Of course he was angry, she thought woozily. It was his house. Nothing had been the same for him since she had arrived. His father had become a recluse, not talking, not answering any questions; his mother had disappeared after an awful row.

And now this.

She sat with her uncle, on the bench outside the kitchen window; the morning sun filtered through the pines, casting long shadows on the lawn.

She did not know what to say to Tristan. His voice was barely audible, his face lined and drained, his hands shaking.

'It's my fault,' he was mumbling.

Summer thought for a horrible moment that he was talking about the fire.

Then he said, 'I shouted at him. Raged at him. The way he was with you – laying into you like that, screaming that you had started the fire. He was crazy. I told him to get out of my sight. And now he has.'

'It's not your fault,' Summer protested. 'You can't blame him. I would hate me if I were him,' she added quietly.

Tristan shook his head and reached out and touched her hand. 'Don't.'

'But it's true, of course it is. I've ruined everything. You were all fine before I came along—'

'The way I see it, we wouldn't be here at all if it weren't for you,' Tristan said. 'We might have been burned to death.'

Summer shuddered. She remembered sitting outside, being checked over for smoke inhalation, wrapped in blankets afterwards, sipping hot tea. A fire officer had spoken to her: 'You and your uncle did well. We got here in time to save the place. Incredible, really. All that wood in the panels on the walls and the staircases; could have been a towering inferno in no time.'

It's not down to me. I was warned.

'It wasn't because of me. You would have – you would have heard the phone . . . and the clock,' she said.

'What?' Tristan looked puzzled.

'The phone – it was ringing and ringing. It – it even carried on when I answered it. Maybe the fire had damaged the line upstairs somewhere . . . and the clock, it wouldn't stop chiming.'

Tristan was shaking his head. 'No, I don't think so.'

Summer felt nauseous as something occurred to her.

It was just like a fire alarm.

Then she remembered the cat's behaviour. It had tried to tell her too. She nearly asked Tristan if it was OK – she had not seen it since the night before. She stopped herself, realizing Tristan had enough on his mind already.

'I – I can't believe you didn't hear the noise,' she persisted. 'The clock went on and on.'

Tristan looked at her curiously. 'That clock hasn't worked for years. Not since—' He bit his lip. 'Not since Becca and I moved here,' he said haltingly.

Summer shook her head. She was not making this up. She had heard it.

Tristan had gone back into himself, staring at his hands, silent and unreachable.

Summer thought again about the evening before. She had toyed with the idea of going up to the attic, hadn't she? She might have been there earlier to stop a fire spreading. Or maybe she would have been caught up in it. The nosebleed had preoccupied her. She had been upset by the memory of her mum.

Had that been a warning too? And the car over-

heating . . . Mum? What are you trying to say?

No, she was letting the shock get to her. She was linking things that had nothing in common. Reading into things.

But what if they *had* all been linked? What if they had been a warning that had become more and more insistent, until she had had to take notice?

Why would Mum want the attic to burn?

It was ridiculous. She tried to talk sense into herself.

'Did – did they say how they thought the fire had started?' she asked Tristan.

His head jerked up, startled out of his reverie. 'Oh, an electrical fault, the fire service reckons,' he murmured. 'The police say that, at first glance, they very much doubt foul play.

Kenan thinks it's foul play.

Tristan went on with a sigh, 'They will have to look into it, of course. For insurance, and everything. Poor old Bosleven. There's always something: leaking roof, bad electrics. Hardly surprising in a place this old.'

Summer remembered the footsteps she had heard. Had someone started the fire on purpose?

'If we're going to blame anyone, it should be me,' Tristan said. 'All those books and papers up in the attic. They were perfect tinder. Becca was always telling me to clear it out. But – oh, I know, stupid and sentimental, isn't it? – there were a lot of photos and things up there.

227

Memories that I don't really want to . . .' His face was suddenly so sad.

The photos!

Why hadn't she taken them while she had had the chance? She should ask him now. Although, without them as evidence, he could deny those particular ones ever existed. She plunged in.

'Talking of photos—'

Through the open window, the hall phone sliced through her words, sending her blood cold.

Every time I try to ask him, something interrupts us!

Tristan jumped up. 'Phone still works, at least,' he called over his shoulder as he climbed through the enormous open window behind them, taking a short cut through the kitchen to answer the call.

Summer got up and leaned through the window, straining to catch Tristan's voice. She heard: '. . . goodness . . . fetch him? . . . OK.' Then a silence as the caller clearly spoke at length and Tristan listened.

He came to the window shortly, his face drawn. He leaned against the frame, as though he needed the support.

'Found him,' he said.

Kenan.

Summer felt her heart fly to her throat.

'Is he – he's all right?'

Tristan nodded, his mouth set in a thin line.

She sat down on the back of the bench. 'So?' she said. 'So he's safe.'

Summer let out a long breath. 'Are you – are you going to go and get him? I mean . . . where is he?'

'He's not coming back. He and Becca have decided to find somewhere else to stay.' His tone was weary.

'For now, you mean?' Summer frowned.

Tristan shook his head. 'She's not coming back. And nor is he. It doesn't much matter. We can't stay here either. Not now. I'll need to see about insurance, repairs, not to mention getting somewhere for you and me to stay for a while . . .'

Summer could not speak. What did he mean, 'She's not coming back'? Her aunt had not been at Bosleven for the whole time Summer had come to live there.

Suddenly Summer felt uncontrollably angry at this man who always allowed himself to be pushed around by his son – and his wife, it seemed – who was so calm, so accepting of everything that had happened. He should be screaming, raging at the loss of his family, the damage to his home.

'Always liked a bit of a drama, Kenan,' Tristan muttered.

That did it. Summer found her voice, spiked with fury: 'A *bit* of a drama? A BIT of a drama? Dragging me by the hair while a fire rages above him, blaming me for it? Running away so you're beside yourself? Are you EVER going to tell me what's going on—?'

'OK, I'll admit, Kenan's made quite a statement.'

'Dooooh!' Summer slammed her fist on the bench beside her in exasperation.

Tristan jumped at the noise and finally looked Summer in the eye for the first time.

She crossed her arms tightly across her chest and held his gaze, challenging him.

'Will you please tell me what is going on?' she said. 'Why doesn't your wife want me here? Why haven't I met her? Please—!'

Tristan held out a hand to stop her. 'You're right. I have to. Explain. Stay here a minute. I need to show you something.' He turned away from the window and walked into the shadows of the house.

Summer went inside and waited in the kitchen for her uncle to return. The air was sharp with smoke and acrid odours from the burned house.

When, after some time, Tristan did come back, he was carrying something in both hands, keeping it close to his body as though it were incredibly fragile.

For one heart-stopping moment Summer thought it was the cat, but it was the tin box she had found in the attic.

Tristan set the box down on the kitchen table. It was even more battered than it had been and blackened by the fire.

'The one thing I would have loved to see go up in flames,' he said, nodding at the tin. 'And the only thing they saved. From all that . . . junk.' He was talking to himself now. 'She always had a way of getting through to me. I can see it now. Her final act.'

Summer gasped. 'What do you mean?'

Tristan smiled sadly. 'You mentioned photos, and I knew you'd found them. I couldn't face talking about her. I kept trying to avoid it, hoping that you would stop trying to piece things together, that it would all go away. In the end she wouldn't let me be . . . It had to come out in the end. She always said she could never leave Bosleven. Anyway, it's all in here.' He tapped the lid of the box lightly, averting his gaze. 'Everything you need to know. I . . . I can't watch you read it. I'm sorry. I know you'll hate me. I've lost everything now, though, so it doesn't much matter what you think.'

He backed away from the table.

'I'm going to go and talk to Kenan and Becca. I'm sorry, but I can't take you with me. We'll speak later. I – I don't know what else to say just now. I'll leave you to it.'

He turned and walked out of the room without looking back.

Summer thought back to that rainy afternoon in the attic. The cat had been there. It had acted weirdly, just as it had before last night's fire. Had it been trying to tell her something about the contents of the box just as she now believed it had tried telling her about the fire?

Don't be stupid. It's a cat.

She wondered again where the animal was. It seemed to know how to look after itself, though, coming and going as it pleased. It must have run to safety.

She stroked the lid of the tin and swallowed.

Tristan had said she should 'read' it all.

Letters. Must be.

She swallowed again, feeling suddenly very thirsty.

She got up and went to the sink, took an upturned glass from the draining board and filled it from the tap, drinking the water down in harsh gulps.

Returning to the box, she prised open the buckled lid and, as she did so, had a sharp sensation, a vision almost, that she was standing on the edge of a cliff, as she had done with Zach only the previous day.

She closed her eyes for a second and remembered talking to Zach about what it would be like to jump. How she had thought that one small step would mean she was lost forever. One small action now – opening the box – could change everything.

Zach. I wish you were here with me.

Would he have heard about the fire? Would the news have reached the village?

She opened her eyes. This leap would take her where she had thought she wanted to go – to answers and certainty. Did she really want that now? Once she jumped, there would be not the slightest chance of scrabbling back to the safety of unknowing.

The past was here, beneath her fingers. She thought of Zach's gran, telling her not to keep her mother locked out, but to listen, to open the door.

'That's the only way you'll find out what it is she wants you to know.'

She sat down, slid the box closer to her and looked at the photos, neatly stacked in the old tin. Summer did not want to see them just at that moment. She lifted them out and put them to one side and saw an envelope at the bottom of the box. Yellowed and dirty at the edges, as though it had been read over and over.

The handwriting was as familiar to Summer as her own.

Only one letter?

She picked it up. It was thin, insubstantial; not at all important-looking. She turned it over and saw that it had been slit carefully and deliberately with a knife, not torn at in a hurry. She slipped her fingers and thumb into the opening and gently withdrew the letter inside. It was comprised of two small sheets of foxed white paper.

She unfolded it with shaking hands and read:

Dear Triss,

I don't suppose you thought you would
hear from me again. I wanted to speak to
you face to face, but in the end I couldn't.
I'm a coward, I suppose.

There's no way to break this to you
gently. You have a daughter. Don't worry.
I don't want your help and I definitely
don't want your money. I even thought
about not telling you, but then I didn't
think that was fair.

She was born last night and she is
the most beautiful creature. She has big
blue eyes and her lips are like a little
rosebud, waiting to bloom. She is her
father's daughter, I think, although the
midwife swears she's the spit of me - 'the
spit' - it's what Mrs Pendred used to say
about me and Becca, isn't it? I've called
her Summer: Summer Lamorna. Summer
for the summer we had. Lamorna for the
nearest beach to our beach. Our rocky beach
with no name.

I knew we would never last. I saw
the way you looked at Becca when you

thought I wasn't looking. If I had known about the baby sooner, I would have said something. Then you told me it was Becca you loved, and I knew I couldn't tell you. I wanted to keep her. More than I wanted you, by then. I was so angry with you.

I know I've really messed up now because I'll never be able to come back to Bosleven, and I love that place almost more than I love you.

How could I be so selfish? You have to understand: I had to make a clean break. Becca would have known. (She would definitely know now if she could see Summer.)

The only way to make sure Becca did not try and stay in touch was to have the row. I didn't drop you in it, and of course I didn't mention the baby. I simply told her I hated her for taking you away from me. Which of course was partly true, but not true enough to make me walk away from my sister and Bosleven. That was the sacrifice I had to make, to protect my sister and my daughter. Myself too, I suppose.

I'm sorry. I know she hates me now:

what's worse, she thinks her twin sister hates her.

She couldn't be more wrong.

I have one thing to ask you. It will probably never be necessary, and I know I am being morbid, but I've decided I want to name you as Summer's guardian. I can't bear the thought of what might happen to this tiny girl if one day I can't be there for her. If anything happened to me I would want her to know her father. And Bosleven is her real home. It's where she came from. She belongs there.

I won't put your name on the birth certificate. I won't mention you as her father in the will either. I've even changed my surname. I'm just plain old Catherine Jones now.

I hope you will feel you can do this one thing for me. For Summer.

Please burn this letter along with the photos.

C x

Summer stared at the pages long after she had finished reading, her eyes opaque with tears.

She knew she should be feeling something towards

her mother for keeping this from her. Anger. Hatred. Betrayal. Disgust, even. She did not feel any of those things. The only thought that swam in and out of her mind was that she was not alone any more. She had a father. Bosleven was her home.

'She belongs there.'

Zach's grandmother had been right: her mother had reached her. Through the thin places. Through the walls of this old house, through the shadows, she had persisted, on and on until the truth had come out.

Then she gasped as something else occurred to her. Kenan. He was . . .

NO!

Her brother.

She dropped the letter on the table as though scorched by it.

But he hates me! Was that why . . . ? Does he know?

She pressed the heels of her hands into her eyes.

His mother. That argument . . .

She made to leave the room and then stopped. She had no idea what to do next. She grabbed the photos from the table and flopped into the old armchair by the dresser. What if Tristan wanted her to go now? What if he could not bear for her to stay another day at Bosleven?

I don't want to leave.

It hit her as she sifted through the images: her mother

had lived here, had loved it, had said Bosleven was Summer's 'real home'.

Is that why I keep seeing her? Feeling her? Hearing things?

Then she remembered what her mother had said in the letter.

'. . . "the spit" – it's what Mrs Pendred used to say about me and Becca . . .'

Kenan had said his mum had been back to get things . . .

Maybe it was not her mother she had seen at all.

Suddenly there was only one person she wanted to talk to.

Zach. I have to tell him.

Chapter Twenty-three

As Summer ran down to the sea, she knew she should have waited and spoken to Tristan. He would come back, see she had gone and think she had run away too, as Kenan had done.

She could not face him, though. Not right away. She had to get things straight. Had to speak to Zach.

He was not on the beach. She scanned the cove. Maybe he had climbed to the Point. Maybe he was fishing. Maybe he had heard about the fire. Would he try to find her at the house?

It was cold. The morning sun had given way to a leaden sky, thick with cloud that had raced inland on a stiff breeze. The air was damp, metallic, threatening rain.

Summer was wild. Her head was spinning from what she had read and her heart was racing from running down to the cliffs. She did not know what she felt any more. She was flailing in a whirlpool of confusion.

An urgent desire took hold of her: to plunge into the water, to wash everything out of her, to feel clean and fresh and new.

She threw off her clothes and jumped into the sea in her underwear. As she fell through the ink-black water, she thought of letting herself go, of never coming up for air again. It would be the easy thing to do. She would not have to face Tristan or Kenan or Becca. Not have to make any decisions about her future. She fell and fell, her lungs tightening.

Easier to drown than to hurl herself off the cliffs.

What about Zach, though? What would happen if he came down and found her, floating? She saw his heart-shaped face, those blue eyes clouded with panic and fear. He did not deserve that.

Tristan did not deserve it either.

She pushed up, up to the surface again and gulped at the cold air, swimming quickly to the side, looking about her again, willing Zach to appear. He would know what to say. What she should do.

Please come. Please.

Still no one.

She heaved herself out of the choppy water and quickly found a foothold on the rough rocks. She knew all the steps and ledges now as well as if she had been climbing over them all her life. She swept up her top and rubbed her arms vigorously with it, then flung it about her shoulders, an ineffective barrier against the chill in the air.

A buzzing, tingling sensation crept through her: it was

not real warmth, only her body going numb, but she did not care. She could not go back until she had spoken to Zach.

'Think you're so cool, don't you?'

She turned her head a fraction, enough to register who was there, but not enough to encourage him to come any nearer.

'Don't think I haven't been watching you,' Kenan shouted, raising his voice. The wind was rising, bringing with it the beginnings of a stormy shower.

Summer felt a few drops fall on her still damp skin. She turned back to look at the water.

What should I do? Swim away from him?

'I'm talking to *you*!' Kenan yelled.

Summer turned to face him squarely. His teeth were bared in an animal snarl. She remembered him pulling her by the hair and felt a jolt of fear.

He's going to thump me.

'Hey, OK,' she said, holding out a hand to keep Kenan at bay. 'I know you're mad at me. But you have to believe it wasn't me. The police said . . . Hey!'

Kenan was coming closer, his eyes narrowed.

I should tell him. That I'm his sister. That I wouldn't hurt him or his mum or anyone.

'We're going to sort this out, just you and me,' Kenan said. He pulled his T-shirt up over his head. Summer saw that the shorts he was wearing were swimming trunks.

'What are you doing?'

He was hardly behaving like a boy getting changed for a casual dip in the sea. He smiled nastily, raising his eyebrows.

'I'm challenging you.'

Summer needed to talk to him calmly, to make him listen. She began wriggling into her top.

'I wouldn't bother doing that,' Kenan said. 'Know why? Because I'm going to race you to the Point. If I win, you have to leave.'

'W-what?' Summer's teeth chattered pathetically against each other. The rain was falling harder now. Her hair was sticking to her cheeks.

'You heard me. I know you reckon you're a fantastic swimmer. You come down here every day with your *boyfriend* – that village *idiot*,' he spat, 'pushing yourself to go further and further. Climbing like a bloody monkey. This is *our* beach. He's not even supposed to be here.'

His words, his tone, his total arrogance: it was as if someone had turned a light on in Summer. A swelling rage rushed through her, hatred charging her with energy.

'You *never* come down here!' Summer shouted.

Kenan's eyes glinted. 'Don't I? How come I know what you've been up to then? You've tried to wheedle your way in since the day you arrived. Mum says you should never have been allowed to set foot in Bosleven.

She says your mum was a slut. A cow.'

Summer roared, chucking her top down and lunging at him, not caring she was in her bra and pants.

He skipped to one side and laughed. 'Let's see who really belongs here, Summer *Jones*.' He paused, raising his eyebrows in challenge. 'We're going to race. To the Point. And when you lose, you'll have to pack up and leave. Go back to where you came from and leave us alone forever. If you don't drown first, that is,' he added. 'But then that would serve you right. *Arsonist*.' He turned and spat on the rocks.

'OK. I'm up for it.' She laughed bitterly. 'Didn't think I'd say that, did you? You'd like to have the guts to get rid of me, but you're too much of a wimp! So you've come up with an idiotic plan. You're going to say we were swimming together, having fun and I had a tragic accident? I don't think so. Like anyone would believe *you*.'

Summer scrambled to the rock's edge. She wasn't going to wait for Kenan, to check he was going to carry out his threat. Part of her felt this could all be a hoax and he was only going to stay on the beach and watch her swim until she couldn't move any more. He was maybe banking on her being too tired, from being up all night. Or too weak.

So what.

Anything, even the knife-sharp thrill of the cold water

against already shivering skin, was better than standing and listening to his taunting.

She plunged in.

'Hey! Wait!' Kenan shouted from the shore.

The cold water made her clench her muscles. She kicked and pushed with determined breaststroke strides until she was out of the Pool and into the bay. The tide was higher now, the water stone-black and forbidding.

A huge splash behind her let Summer know that Kenan had joined her in the water. She wasn't going to waste time in turning to see how fast he was moving. Even if he couldn't carry through his threat of making her go back, he might try to push her under.

That last thought made Summer gasp, inhaling water, the brine stinging her throat. The sea was choppier than it had been earlier. She had to concentrate if she was going to make it the half-mile to the Point.

Her arms were already beginning to feel heavy; the drag of the current made the going hard work. Her hands were losing all feeling in the cold as well, crabbing into claws, the water flowing through her open fingers, slowing her down.

A splashing and gasping behind told her that Kenan was getting closer. She spoke to herself in a stern manner.

Do not panic. You need to conserve energy.

She heard Zach telling her, *'If you focus on your stroke and keep it steady, you'll be there in no time.'*

She had done it before. She would do it again.

He's not gaining on me yet.

Knowing she still had the lead prompted a surge of adrenaline. She looked to her left. She was already halfway across the bay. There were the caves. Those cool dark caves where she'd thought of camping out and hiding when she had first arrived. Where she had lit fires with Zach . . .

A shout pulled her sharply back to the present.

He's trying to distract me. Do not turn around. It's a trick.

'Summer! Stop! I need . . .'

She swam steadfastly on, but Kenan was still shouting. Something about his voice unsettled her.

The rain was heavy now, the noise of it slapping against the waves, the wind whipping the water up, making it harder to see.

Kenan yelled her name. His voice had taken on a different note. It was half swallowed by the sound of the rain falling on the churning water, but Summer knew Kenan was not taunting her any longer.

He was in trouble. He was calling out. For help.

Summer turned and trod water. She half closed her eyes against the sting and splash of the waves and peered back at Kenan. He was thrashing and flailing, barely visible through the grey.

Still, a prickle of unease crept over Summer.

Is he tricking me to go back? Could he really be in difficulty?

She sculled with her stiff hands.

Come on.

She urged her brain into gear.

Make up your mind, quick! If he's really drowning, you can't leave him.

What if this *was* a trap, though? He was devious enough. There was no doubt he'd get away with a story of her drowning through her own stupidity. He would only have to say she had got out of her depth.

'Summeeeeeeeeerrrr!'

His head bobbed above the white spray of a breaking wave for an instant before disappearing beneath the foamy surface. She moved towards him guardedly, to get a better look. Needles of grey bounced off the water, but she could make out the raw terror on Kenan's face, his eyes wide.

'I'm a coward, I suppose.'

Her mother's words swam before her. Her mother had said she had sacrificed her happiness at Bosleven, sacrificed her relationship with her sister too, to keep her, Summer, and to allow Becca and Tristan to be together. She had done this so that they could make a life together, have Kenan. Her brother.

She kicked out and put her face down; threw herself into a powerful front crawl. She knew nothing about life-saving, but felt that if she could just get an arm under him, get his face out of the water, turn him on to his back and at least tell him to shut up and save some energy . . .

'Stop thrashing around!' she yelled, drawing up alongside him.

He wasn't shouting any more. He was whimpering, swallowing water. Bobbing below the surface, hardly bothering to struggle. She had to save him. He could not save himself.

Summer grabbed his arm. 'Listen,' she said sharply. 'Lie on your back and rest your head on my arm.'

He did as she said. She turned on to her back, cupped his chin in her hand to keep his mouth free from the waves and paddled with her free hand so that they were pointing back towards the Pool. They would stand a better chance of getting out there than if they went on to the Point, and they would be closer to home.

Summer knew from her practice swims that distances in the water were deceiving and that the tide could play games with you, tugging you in directions you did not want to go.

'I – I can't go on,' Kenan spluttered.

'Good job I'm here,' she said through gritted teeth.

Kenan surrendered then to Summer's grip.

She made herself picture warm, dry towels and clothes and imagined what it would feel like walking back up to the house – a hike that always warmed her after a bracing, cold swim.

Best not to think about what will happen when we get back.

Kenan had become alarmingly limp: a stuffed toy in her arms. She strained to hear his breathing: it was shallow and rasping.

Summer kicked on, occasionally turning her head a fraction to try and keep on track. She needed to steer as close inland as possible so the tide didn't drag them out. She tried to remember where all the rocks were under the surface so they didn't bash their legs or get caught between any of them.

Something slimy brushed her foot; she shuddered.

Kenan squealed and jerked suddenly.

She grasped him more tightly and snapped, 'Seaweed!'

He fell quiet again, and Summer swam on, his weakness feeding her own strength.

The wind whipped up the surface of the water, working it into rolling breakers which buffeted and tossed the pair of them around.

It was one thing to sit in safety on the rocks and gaze dreamily at a raging sea and marvel at its power. Swimming in it while holding on to someone else was altogether different. Summer pushed away the creeping sensation of fear and focused instead on digging deep whenever a wave rolled towards them.

Just think about reaching land. Land. Land. Land . . .

The waves swept over their heads and they surfaced, spluttering and coughing; Kenan had grabbed Summer's arm and his fingernails sank into her skin. It was a strange kind of comfort to feel the sharp bite against her flesh.

They weren't going to make it with her dragging him along like a lump of useless ballast. She needed to turn on to her front so that she could keep the Pool in sight and judge the waves better. A false move or a sudden push from a breaker, and they would end up being thrown on to the rocks. Summer kept repeating Zach's words to herself: '. . . *focus on your stroke and keep it steady . . .*'

'Do you think you can turn and put your hands on my shoulders?' she shouted. 'Keep your head up and kick if you can.'

'I . . . I don't know,' Kenan's voice was small and distant, but he managed to turn so that they were both facing their destination.

He gripped Summer's shoulders as she doggy-paddled, jutting her chin high to stop herself from swallowing more water.

If we can get to the Pool we'll be OK.

All at once there were voices and a noisy splashing ahead, as someone jumped into the water; a shout of 'I'm coming, don't worry!', and another voice: 'Keep going!

You're nearly in the Pool – just a couple more strokes. We're coming.'

Zach? Tristan too and – someone with them . . .

Summer tried to lift an arm to signal that she had seen them. But her limbs would not respond. A dark blanket of exhaustion drew itself over her; her bones ached with the weight of it.

If I could just sleep, for a little while . . . if I could rest for a couple of minutes . . . I'll just sleep, get my strength back and then . . .

Kenan dropped away from her shoulders as a delicious, warm weight took hold of her.

The sky went black.

Chapter Twenty-four

Summer's eyelids were so heavy. She felt a hand enclose her own. It was warm, soft. She moved her tongue over her teeth. Her mouth was dry, furry, her tongue swollen.

'She's waking up.'

A woman's voice.

Mum?

She strained to force her eyes open, curious to see who was sitting beside her.

A dark, cloudy image swam in front of her, but the light was too bright. She had to close her eyes again.

Am I—? Did I drown?

She struggled to open her eyes again and this time saw long, wavy dark hair framing a face that peered anxiously into hers.

'Get her some water.'

A glass was held to her lips, someone took a firm hold of the back of her head and raised her slowly. She drank. A damp cloth was pressed on her forehead.

*

'I'm sorry.'

Whispered voices.

'I know. Nothing seems . . .' A heavy sigh. 'Nothing's so important now.'

'I . . . I don't know about that.'

Tears, words distorted, voices shaky.

'Kenan . . . I couldn't stop him. I shouldn't have told him.'

'You had to.'

'He said he wanted to kill her.'

'He didn't mean it.'

'I think he did.'

Summer looked into the bright, white light, recognized the features on the face this time.

Mum, but not Mum. Mum as she might be if . . .

Her throat was dry, so dry.

'Can I—?' Her voice was hoarse, not her own.

'Triss! Quick—'

Hands rushed to help her up to sitting. Tristan held her, his arm strong and safe around her back.

Memories. Photos. A letter.

'Dad'. How am I ever going to get used to that?

Pictures of thrashing limbs swam in and out of her mind.

'Kenan!' she cried out.

'It's OK. You're in hospital. Kenan's here too,' Tristan said. 'He's fine.'

'Thanks to you.'

The other voice. Her.

She was helped to more water while pillows were plumped up behind her.

'There you are, sweetheart.'

Summer took a sip, then handed the woman the water glass and sank back.

'That better?' Becca took her hand as she had before and stroked it. A bleak smile flickered on her lips.

'Huh?' Summer croaked. She blinked.

I'm seeing things again. Not real.

Becca's red-rimmed eyes filled with fresh tears. 'Cat's little girl,' she whispered. 'Thank God. Triss and I . . . We thought—'

'You?' Summer whispered. She fought against the woolliness in her head, tried to make sense of what she was seeing and hearing. 'You're . . . All those times . . . I thought it was . . . thought I was seeing things, making it up . . .'

Becca looked puzzled.

Summer licked her dry lips. Trying to explain. 'I kept seeing Mum. I saw her when I was in the garden. I thought I did . . . ?'

Tristan patted her hand. 'Don't try to talk too much too soon.'

Summer had had enough of not talking. She pushed on the pillows, struggled for a more upright position.

'No – listen! I was out in the garden and I saw Mum.' Her voice gathered momentum, in a rush now to get it all out, to be heard. Finally to get the answers she so badly wanted. 'And there was a day I was out – at the Merry Maidens. And another time, I heard the piano – I recognized the piece, one of Mum's favourites. And I saw her – you. Oh! I don't know. The piece it was—'

'Debussy,' said Becca. '"Clair de Lune". My favourite too. I was playing . . .'

'You?'

'I came in from the Wing. I wanted to see if I could get a glimpse of you. I'd tried once before when you were in the garden. Then I thought the house was empty and I missed playing, so . . . I'm sorry. I didn't mean to frighten you.' Becca faltered.

Summer shook her head. 'You were spying on me? All that time I thought I was going crazy, seeing ghosts—!' Her voice rose another notch.

Becca grabbed her wrist with both hands, her face drawn, pleading. 'I'm sorry. I know I was wrong. I was just so angry. At Cat, at the way she had lied. And Triss . . .' Her voice broke. She dropped Summer's hand.

Tristan tried to pull his wife to him, but she shrugged him off. She swallowed. 'I decided to wait, to try and talk to you alone,' she went on. 'So when I saw you that day, going in through the gate to the Merry Maidens, I thought I would grab my chance. I was coming back from

Newlyn. I saw you on that bike. You looked like her. Cat. Then I saw you were with that boy, and when you came running, you looked so upset. I couldn't face it. Especially not in front of someone else.'

'I don't understand,' Summer said. 'I thought you had gone away. How . . . where have you been staying?'

Tristan coughed. He was looking down at his hands, twisting them over and over.

Becca chewed her lip. 'I was staying out of the way, in one of the rooms in the Wing – the unused wing of the house. Pathetic, I know. I needed a bit of space so that I could work things out.' She paused, her expression pained. 'I told them to keep you out of my way until I was ready. It wasn't that I wanted to *leave* exactly. I didn't want to leave Kenan anyway . . .' Her words fell from her in a rush, as though in relief at finally being able to explain.

'So you were in the *house* all the time?' Summer asked.

Becca shook her head. 'Not all the time. I went out a lot. Did a lot of walking. Thinking. I slept in one of the Wing bedrooms. Until our fight.' She looked at Tristan, who was still staring at his hands.

Summer frowned. 'How come I never saw you walking through the house?'

Tristan spoke at last. 'She made us keep the other entrance closed. The door at the end of the kitchen passage downstairs. And the bookcase next to your room – there's a door behind there too. They both go through to the Wing.'

'The books!' Summer gasped.

Tristan looked puzzled. 'What about them?'

Summer felt a hot rush of embarrassment as she pieced things together. 'I saw them move, saw some on the floor once, then someone had put them back – I heard noises, laughter too. I thought . . . I thought it was ghosts again.' It all sounded so ridiculous and garbled now.

'No ghosts – it was me,' said Becca awkwardly. 'I – I know it was wrong, but I went into your room. Then I heard you coming, so I left and—'

'My photo! Of mum!' Summer said. 'So it was you – not Kenan.'

Becca looked so miserable.

'This is my fault,' Tristan put in. 'I told Kenan we didn't want you to know where Becca was,' said Tristan.

Becca reached out and squeezed his hand. 'No, it was me. I told Kenan not to show Summer the Wing. Like I say, I was angry.' She looked at Summer. 'We were both angry, Kenan and me. The Wing was our secret. Our safe place. It was selfish. I'm so sorry.' Her face crumpled as she began to cry softly.

Summer's head was swimming. 'I heard you argue. About me.'

'I know. I should never have said those things,' Becca sobbed. 'It's not as though any of it is your fault.'

Tristan took Summer's hand in his free one.

I have to make him tell me everything.

'But – in that letter – Mum said you didn't know. That she had left before . . .' she stumbled, uncomfortable.

'I . . . I think I did know,' Tristan said quietly. 'I was foolish. Young. Selfish too.'

'It's all over,' Becca said. She wiped at her tears. 'It was so long ago. Cat was the one who paid the price, cutting herself off from me, leaving Triss, Bosleven, changing her name –' she looked at Summer – 'bringing you up, alone. I couldn't have done that, brought Kenan up on my own.'

Summer felt a rush of pity for the boy. 'Kenan is all right, isn't he? You did say he was?' she asked.

'He's fine. And it really is thanks to you,' Tristan said. 'He's in the next room. You'll both be coming home – I mean—'

Summer interrupted him. 'There is one thing I don't have an answer for.'

The two adults looked at her anxiously.

May as well. Now or never.

She told them, warily, about the phone call the night her mother had died.

Becca's eyes grew large as she listened. 'What time did you say?'

Summer repeated. 'One minute before midnight – the time they say she died.'

Becca drew a sharp breath. 'Exactly the same – the same thing happened at Bosleven. Don't you remember, Triss?'

Tristan nodded. 'It was . . . we couldn't believe it, really.'

Summer waited.

'It woke us,' Becca said. 'You were deeply asleep, Triss. I answered the phone and . . . heard her. I told him about it,' she said to Summer, 'but he wasn't properly awake. When I told him again in the morning, he convinced me I must have been dreaming. Of course I didn't know anything about the accident. I just knew it was Cat. I hadn't spoken to her for fourteen years! And when I tried to say something to her, the line went dead.'

'So when did you find out? That she had died?' Summer asked.

'When the solicitor rang about the will,' said Tristan.

'I had to ask – when did she die, what time,' Becca cut in. 'Then they said – it was exactly when the phone call came through . . .'

More tears.

'Is that when you first knew about me?' Summer whispered.

Becca nodded. 'Tristan had kept it a secret, as Cat had asked him to. So, you see? It was a huge shock. I am sorry, I know you don't want to hear this, but I was so, *so* angry with them both. I was devastated that Cat had died, that I never got the chance to say goodbye, to make things better. I was furious that you . . . I had to tell Kenan. Imagine telling your son that he has a half-sister and that she's coming to live with us, like that, out of the blue!' Her voice rose, the words coming faster, the more distraught she became. 'I couldn't tell him everything at first. I made Triss say that you were his cousin, that we were family and we *had* to look after you. I thought I would be able to handle it, then on the day you were due to arrive, I just locked myself in the Wing. Poor Kenan. I had to tell him then. That Triss was *your* dad too . . . That I couldn't bear it . . . What a mess!' She buried her head in her hands.

Summer did not know what to feel any more. She knew she should feel sorry for Becca – go easy on her, probably – but she still had questions. 'So the phone call? What happened? How did you know it was Mum?'

Becca took a hanky from her sleeve and blew her nose. 'I definitely remember the time of the call – I looked at the radio alarm before I picked up the phone. 23:59. "Who would call at that hour?" I remember thinking that.'

'What did she say?'

Becca let out a shuddering sigh. 'She said, "Bye, love."' Her face creased up again. She wept. 'It's how

259

she always used to say goodbye.'

Summer went cold. 'That's what she said to me too,' she said.

She heard Zach's gran again.

'Grief can open doors that would normally be firmly held closed.'

'She found her way back,' said Becca, smiling through her tears. 'Through you. She's come home. And she's brought you home too. Bosleven is your home, you know that?'

Summer turned the words over in her mind.

Home. Bosleven. Home.

They sounded good together. She pictured the old house, no longer spooky in her mind's eye; the rambling gardens; the rockery and that beautiful beach. Why would she want to live anywhere else? Then she remembered something.

'I've been meaning to ask. Is the little white cat all right?' she said.

Tristan and Becca both frowned. 'What cat?' they choroused.

'The little white cat,' Summer repeated. 'I never asked you its name. It's always coming and going – hardly sits still for a second! I tried looking at its tag once. It was quite worn. All I could see was the letter "C"—'

'What . . . Sorry, I don't know what you're talking about,' Becca cut in, perplexed.

It was Summer's turn to look puzzled. 'But it was in the house. I assumed it was yours . . . it was always there, running around. I followed it up to the attic one time. That's when I found the photos. And the night of the fire – the cat went ballistic. I did think at the time it was trying to tell me something—' She stopped short.

Tristan and Becca both looked white with shock.

'We've never had a cat,' Tristan said quietly.

Epilogue

'You knew?' Summer repeated in disbelief.

Zach concentrated on casting his line and did not turn to face her.

'Gran told me,' he said. 'Only after the fire, though. I didn't know anything before that, I swear.'

'Why didn't you find me, *tell* me? You knew how freaked out I'd been by everything. All that stuff your gran said. She made me carry on believing I'd been seeing ghosts.' She wanted to be angry at him.

'I . . . I'm sorry,' said Zach, finally raising his eyes from the line. 'Gran said we should stay out of it. She knew there had been . . . bad times in the family. She said the whole village knew about the twins – your mum and Becca. They knew about the fight they had, the fact that your mum left Bosleven. Then, when Becca married Tristan and they took on the house, they just kind of shut themselves away there. Kept things private. Anyway,' he added, bracing himself as he felt a tug on the line, 'she didn't "make" you believe anything. She believes in those things: spirits, the thin places . . .' He started reeling in his catch. 'I believe in those things too. I think when I die, there'll be part of me that stays right here.'

Summer stared pensively as the fish came up, wriggling on the hook. Had she been reeled in by a load of fanciful stories?

If so, how could she ever explain the way she and Becca had both received the same call, the same words spoken at the exact time of her mother's death? What about the fire, that picture she had of her mother lying in a pool of blood while her own nose bled? She *knew* those had been warnings; she just knew. Even Tristan had said so. The clock that had not worked since Becca and Tristan had got together – since her mum had left . . . and that one box – how come it survived when everything else in the attic had been destroyed? It was too weird. As though her mum had had enough of Tristan skirting the issue, not being straight with her, and had decided to take things into her own hands, burning everything away to leave the evidence laid bare, for all to see.

'Then there was that cat,' Summer said.

Zach looked at her. 'What?'

'Sorry, I was just thinking things through – strange things have happened to me ever since I've arrived here. One of the most bizarre is there was always this little white cat, leading me here to the beach, leading me to find photos of my mum, and then trying to tell me about the fire. I haven't seen it since.'

'Cat?' Zach said.

With that one word, it was as though a veil had been drawn back.

'Cat – Catherine,' she whispered. 'Mum . . .'

She looked across to the Point.

'So what will you do? Now you know the truth?' Zach was unhooking the fish but was watching her closely. He put it in the bucket at his feet. 'Will you – stay?' He cleared his throat. 'I'd like it. If you did.'

Summer slipped her hand into Zach's. He pulled her to him, his bright blue eyes looking deep into hers.

Then, smiling, she said, 'Yes. I'll stay. I've come home, haven't I?'

Acknowledgements

The house, beach, gardens and village in this story are based on real places, but I have altered the names and topography to keep them private. Some other places, such as the Merry Maidens, Newlyn and of course Penzance, are real. The people in the book are entirely fictional and not based on anyone I have ever met.

I would like to thank all the members of my family who encouraged me to write this book, which is so different from anything I have written before. The idea came from a family member who knows how much I adore the area of Cornwall I have described. To those who love it as much or even more than I do, I hope I have done it justice.

I would also like to thank the editors and readers without whose help I could not have crafted and shaped the story: Emma Young, Polly Nolan, Rachel Kellehar, Nick de Somogyi, Cathy Hopkins and Fleur Hitchcock. Thank you especially to Hilary Delamere, who read the first draft of the scene where Kenan challenges Summer to race to the Point and pressed me to write more.

Most of all my thanks go to Lucy and David, who enjoyed early drafts of *Summer's Shadow* and kept me going with their love and their belief in me.